"I don't know  **Nathaniel Stalli... to you and me...**

He took a step closer to her, shifting his weight and warmth nearer to her. He clasped her hands between his own, entwining their fingers together. "It's like you were saying last night. The bond between us is practically sacred. You are as much a joy and a blessing in my life as I am in yours. We're good together and it has scared the hell out of us both. But it's time we stopped being scared. We're missing out on the best thing that could happen to either of us. And like you said, I don't want to miss out on anything more."

A slow upward bend of Rebecca's mouth made her entire face glow. She nodded slowly. "So you did hear what I said last night."

"I heard every word, Bec."

She bit down against her bottom lip. "So what now?"

A low gust of air blew past his full lips. Nathaniel lifted her hands and kissed the backs of her fingers. His touch was gentle, his lips like silk against her skin as he kneaded the flesh softly.

Dear Reader,

Temptation always leads to trouble, as Nathaniel Stallion quickly discovers with his favorite girl, the one and only Rebecca Marks. Best friends, neither anticipates their friendship becoming anything more. But much more can't help but happen when these two try to fight their attraction to each other.

I really love this story! I love it as much as Nathaniel loves Rebecca—the full-figured beauty giving him all kinds of feel good! And of course, he's a Stallion, and Stallion men are everything AND a bag of chips!

Thank you so much for your support of my Kimani title and of all my writing. I am humbled by all the love you keep showing me, my characters and our stories. I know that none of this would be possible without you.

Until the next time, please take care, and may God's blessings be with you always.

With much love,

Deborah Fletcher Mello

www.deborahmello.blogspot.com

TO TEMPT A *Stallion*

DEBORAH FLETCHER MELLO

⬥ **HARLEQUIN**® KIMANI™ ROMANCE

Recycling programs
for this product may
not exist in your area.

ISBN-13: 978-1-335-21658-8

To Tempt a Stallion

HARLEQUIN®
www.Harlequin.com

Printed in U.S.A.

Writing since forever, **Deborah Fletcher Mello** can't imagine herself doing anything else. Her first novel, *Take Me to Heart*, earned her a 2004 Romance Slam Jam nomination for Best New Author. In 2008, Deborah won the RT Reviewers' Choice award for Best Series Romance for her ninth novel, *Tame a Wild Stallion*. Deborah received a BRAB 2015 Reading Warrior Award for Best Series for her Stallion family series. Deborah was also named the 2016 Romance Slam Jam Author of the Year. She has also received accolades from several publications, including *Publishers Weekly*, *Library Journal* and *RT Book Reviews*. With each new book, Deborah continues to create unique story lines and memorable characters. Born and raised in Connecticut, Deborah now considers home to be wherever the moment moves her.

Books by Deborah Fletcher Mello

Harlequin Kimani Romance

Visit the Author Profile page
at Harlequin.com for more titles.

To the Bubster!
Your energy is so infectious!
Thank you for bringing me so much joy!
I love that no matter what,
you always make me SMILE!

Chapter 1

The ballpoint pen in Nathaniel Stallion's right hand shook ever so slightly as his real estate agent pointed out each line on the purchase contract where he needed to sign. With each Post-it arrow, the lot of them multicolored in neon pink, orange, yellow and blue, which she removed after he'd inked his name, his heart beat a little faster.

Twenty minutes later he was the proud owner of the prettiest piece of real estate in Carmel, California. The property was perched on one of the world's most iconic stretches of coastline. With pristine views of the Monterey Peninsula and the Pacific Ocean, it was the ideal spot for his newest business venture and it was all his.

Nicholas Stallion wheeled himself around the table

to shake his twin brother's hand. "Congratulations! I'm very excited for you," he said as he locked his wheelchair in place.

Nathaniel took a deep breath to steel the last of his nervousness. "Thank you," he said, his own smile galvanizing. "Now the real work begins. I only have six weeks before the grand opening."

Nicholas laughed. "Only you would buy a restaurant and only give yourself a month and a half to renovate and reopen!"

"Natalie would do that, too!"

"Yeah, but you know better. Our baby sister has always been impulsive."

Elise Montgomery gave them both a bright smile. The former fashion model was Carmel's leading real estate agent and her exuberance over the six-figure commission she'd just earned had her beaming like an LED lightbulb. "Well, this is definitely cause for celebration!" she exclaimed excitedly. A tray holding crystal flutes seemed to appear out of nowhere. Elise popped the cork on a bottle of champagne.

The two men watched as she filled the flutes with bubbly, passing them both a glass. "Congratulations," she said, lifting her own glass in salute. "May you have a lifetime of prosperity with your newest venture."

"Hear! Hear!" Nicholas echoed before taking a small sip of the beverage.

"So tell me," Elise said as she set her glass down on the table. "Do you two call each other in the mornings to plan your attire?" She looked from one to the other, pointing out their identical polo shirts and matching slacks.

Nathaniel laughed. "Never! It's our twin thing. We have the same tastes and shop in the same stores."

"Even when we try not to dress alike, we dress alike," Nicholas finished.

Laughter rang warmly through the conference room.

"I really need to get something to eat," Nicholas said as he put his still full glass onto the conference table. It's a little early for me and I have to take my meds."

"Would you like to join us for lunch?" Nathaniel questioned, turning his gaze toward Elise.

"I actually have another closing in two hours so I'll have to pass, but maybe you and I could finish this bottle of champagne later over dinner?" Her eyebrows were raised suggestively.

Nicholas smiled. "I think I'll get a head start toward the car," he said. He extended his hand. "Elise, it was a pleasure to meet you."

"The pleasure was mine. I hope we'll see each other again soon. I'd love to meet your wife. I've heard wonderful things about her."

"Tarah is an amazing woman," Nicholas said. "I look forward to you two getting to know each other." He winked an eye at his brother. "I'll see you outside."

Nathaniel nodded. "I'm right behind you," he said as Nicholas rolled himself out the door. When his twin was out of sight he turned his attention back to the woman who was still eyeing him like he was a slab of meat for the taking.

Elise took a step closer to him, drawing her palm against his chest. "So, what about that dinner?"

"I wish I could," he said, his tone apologetic. "But I really won't have any down time for the next few weeks. Too much to do. I'm actually meeting with the contractor this evening. Can I get a rain check?"

Disappointment washed over Elise's face. She took a deep breath. "You owe me, Nathaniel Stallion. I think this is the third time you've turned me down."

Nathaniel chuckled. He took a step back and crossed his arms over his chest. "You scare me, Elise. I'm not ready for a serious relationship and you want a husband."

She laughed. "I'm sure if we give it some thought, Mr. Stallion, we can come to a happy medium. Something like best friends with privileges, maybe?" Her coquettish expression was teasing as she batted her eyelashes at him.

Nathaniel shook his head ever so slightly. "I need to run. I will call you and maybe then we can make plans."

"Promise?"

"We'll see," he said as he winked his eye at her and headed for the door. "Have a good afternoon, Elise!"

Minutes later Nathaniel and his brother were laughing heartily together. They sat at a corner table in Dametra Café, dining on fried calamari, dolmas, spanakopita and moussaka. The cozy restaurant with its assortment of Mediterranean cuisine was one of their favorites and the two brothers ate there every time Nicholas came to visit.

"Why don't you just tell that woman you're not interested?" Nicholas asked.

Nathaniel shrugged his broad shoulders. "Because I might be interested once I get my head clear. Right now though I have too much on my mind. The restaurant, my medical practice, you."

"What are you worried about me for?"

"Someone needs to worry about you. You don't worry enough and you should."

"I have a wife for that, and trust me, she does a great job."

"I know. It's why I call her regularly to check up on you."

"So then you already know what the doctors have said about my next surgery."

"I know it's a clinical trial with no certainty for success."

"Well, life doesn't promise you certainty. Besides, they're just going to implant an electrode stimulator along my spinal cord, flip the switch and then see what happens. We'll keep our fingers crossed and say a lot of prayer."

"As long as you understand this research is still in its early stages. I don't want you to be disappointed if you don't get the results you want."

"I'd be disappointed if I didn't give it a try. So I'm good with it."

The two stared at each other. Nathaniel carried much guilt about his brother's condition. Nicholas, a former professional football player, had been severely injured in the biggest championship game of his career. Years before his accident, Nathaniel had warned him of the risks, pointing out that previous trauma had already left Nicholas more susceptible to injury. Back then he had recommended that Nicholas retire, but always stubborn, his brother had refused. Nathaniel should have insisted but he'd supported his twin's choice instead. Now, Nicholas was a paraplegic, permanently confined to a wheel chair, and Nathaniel felt partially responsible.

"Don't do that," Nicholas said.

"Do what?"

"Make me feel bad. We're supposed to be celebrating and you're making me feel bad. Now I'm depressed." Nicholas grinned. "Not really!"

"Sorry," Nathaniel said with a chuckle. He held up both hands as if he were surrendering. "Changing the subject. So, catch me up with the family. I've been ignoring your sisters so I know they're pissed at me."

"Pissed doesn't begin to express what those two are feeling right now. I'm supposed to dial them both while I'm here with you since you won't call either of them back."

Nathaniel laughed. "Naomi left a vicious message. Marriage clearly hasn't sweetened her pleasant disposition."

"Patrick definitely has his hands full with her. But she and Natalie just want to know you're okay. Natalie and Tinjin are planning to fly in next month, I think."

"I'll call them both this evening. I swear I will."

"Have you talked to Noah?"

"Not since last month when I told him about buying the property. He's planning to come help with my security systems."

"Well, let him tell you before you say anything, but he and Catherine are pregnant! He told me yesterday and I'm sure he wants to tell you himself."

"Hot damn!" Nathaniel exclaimed. "We're going to be uncles!"

Nicholas laughed with his brother. "It's pretty cool right? I never imagined any of us having kids. A week ago it seemed like such a foreign concept and now I'm excited. For them and us."

"You and Tarah haven't thought about kids?"

"We talk about it all the time. But she says she's not ready and right now, with my situation, well…" He shrugged slightly.

Nathaniel nodded his understanding. He moved the conversation forward. "The last time I talked to Natalie she said the same thing. She and Tinjin weren't ready yet."

"When I talked to her she said they want to open their New York office and settle down in a home here in the United States before taking that step."

"I really don't see Natalie leaving Paris."

"Me, either, but you never know. She may be missing this crazy, dysfunctional family of ours!"

"Speaking of dysfunctional, have you spoken to Nolan?" Nathaniel asked, referring to the wayward father they had all just recently begun to have a relationship with.

Nolan Perry was the biological parent who had not been in their lives when they were children. For too many years to count Nolan had been their mother's lover, impregnating the teenaged Norris Jean Stallion while he claimed a wife and family on the other side of the Utah town where they'd been raised. Five children later, he'd blown out of their lives like a gale-force wind, leaving the twins and their siblings broken like downed trees.

Just a few short months before their sister Naomi's wedding, they all discovered Nolan had been as deceived and betrayed as they had been. Blatant lies, half-truths and seriously bad choices had kept him from his children, and now he was making a genuine effort to make up for lost time.

Nicholas nodded. "He's coming to help out when I have my surgery." He shifted his eyes up to look directly at his brother. "He volunteered to come stay with me so Tarah doesn't have to miss any time from the hospital. He's also excited about coming for your grand opening."

"It's still weird to me that we have a father who actually wants to be a part of our lives. I'm still not sure how I feel about it."

"I know, right? But it's all good. No matter what, we still have each other. Stallions for life!"

Nathaniel grinned. "Stallions for life!"

The duo talked for another hour, falling into a rhythm they'd known since the womb. Nathaniel was excited to share his plans with his twin. Nicholas was proud of his brother and his added exuberance had them both riding sky-high.

Nathaniel suddenly cussed. "What time is it?" he asked as he tapped at his wristwatch, the device still reading nine-thirty. He looked around the room, the lunch crowd having disappeared almost entirely.

"It's just four-thirty. Bad battery?"

"More like time for a new watch. But I need to run. I'm meeting Bec and the contractor at the new property."

"Bec? Rebecca's here in town?" Nicholas eyed him with a raised brow. "When did that happen?"

"She flew in this morning. Why are you looking at me like that?"

Nicholas laughed. "Oh my, my, my! No wonder your real estate agent couldn't get any play from you. I can't wait to tell your sisters this!"

Nathaniel shook his head. "Please, don't start. I've just hired Bec and her firm to do the marketing and promotion for the restaurant. That's all."

His twin brother grinned. "If you say so! You do know what your sisters say about Rebecca, don't you?"

"Yeah," Nathaniel responded as he laid cash on the table for the tab. "They say too damn much and they're wrong, as usual!"

Nicholas laughed. "I definitely won't tell them you said that!"

Rebecca Marks walked the perimeter of the 17-Mile Drive property to stare out at the magnificent views.

The 3600-square-foot building was a fusion of glass and natural stone, blending seamlessly into the landscape. She loved everything about it. The foreclosure property was even more stupendous than Nathaniel had described. After seeing it up close and personal she completely understood his obsession. And knowing his dream she felt he was a step closer to his goal. Everything about that warmed her heart.

She and Nathaniel had been best buddies since the two had been freshmen at UCLA. They'd become each other's confidantes, sidekicks and go-to pals for practically everything. Over the years they'd found an easy balance with each other that worked for them both. But truth be told, Rebecca had been head over heels in love with Nathaniel since the day she'd first laid eyes on him. Nathaniel had never looked at her with a romantic eye but their friendship and unyielding bond had been motivation enough to drop everything when he'd called and asked for her help.

Only Rebecca knew how difficult the past two years had actually been for him. His twin brother's accident had taken a toll on his spirit. His father suddenly appearing in his life and wanting a relationship had stressed him immensely. Dealing with it all while still trying to maintain his medical practice had almost been too much for him to handle. Emotionally, he'd been fractured and desperate not to let it show. There had been many late-night calls between them when Nathaniel had shared what he was feeling, trusting the advice he knew she would give.

When he'd shared his desire to open a restaurant, pursuing a long-held dream of being a successful restaurateur, she'd been the first to encourage him to go for it. Others had laughed, some claiming he was ranting like a man in a midlife crisis. Nathaniel had never been known to take risks. Nor had he often stepped out of his comfort zone. He was a renowned orthopedic surgeon, one of the best in his field. His practice, which specialized in sports medicine, serviced many high-profile clients. He'd invested his money wisely over the years and had a sizeable bank balance to fall back on. He had absolutely nothing to lose, so why not do something that would make him happy. *You only live once*, Rebecca had insisted as she'd purposely tripped him toward the unknown and what she hoped would prove to be his destiny.

When he'd called to say he had decided to take a lengthy hiatus from medicine to take that leap of faith, and needed her help, she'd been excited for the opportunity. Excited to see him spreading his wings and allowing her to join him on the journey. And flying to Carmel meant being right by his side as he fulfilled his dream, even if it was only for a short time. Since buying the house in Carmel, Nathaniel had been spending less time in Los Angeles and although they spoke often, she missed their one-on-one interaction. She missed him, even if she didn't say so out loud.

Lost in reverie, Rebecca jumped when Nathaniel suddenly stepped in behind her, wrapping his arms around her torso. A low squeal blew past her lips, replacing the scream that teased the back of her throat. She slapped at him lightly as he laughed.

"Boo!" Nathaniel exclaimed as he pulled her into a deep bear hug.

"You just scared the crap out of me, Nathaniel Stallion!" she said as she punched him again. "You're so lucky you didn't get maced."

He leaned to kiss her cheek, his arms still holding her tightly. "Sorry about that. I couldn't resist."

"You're too damn old to be playing games like that, Stallion."

He laughed again. "I'm not that old."

Rebecca shook her head. "Where's Nicholas? I thought you two were together?"

"He had to fly back to LA so I dropped him off at the airport before I came here."

"Shoot! I hate that I missed him! How's he doing?"

"He's good. He's really good, actually. I told you about the surgery, didn't I?"

"You did. And he's good with everything?"

"Better than I am, probably. I still have some concerns."

"Concerns like…?"

There was a moment of hesitation as Nathaniel dropped into thought before he answered. "I sometimes think he's only looking for a miracle because others want one for him. Him walking again is more important to everyone else than to him and it's the only reason he keeps putting himself through the stuff he does. I only want the best for him and I think he'd be happier if he never had to see another doctor again. He and Tarah are incredible together and he's comfortable and happy with the life they have."

"Have you talked to him about it?"

"Not really. Not like I should."

"Talk to him. You keep waiting for the right time and it might never come, so just do it. Tell him how you feel. It'll make you feel better."

With a quick nod, Nathaniel changed the subject. "So how was your flight?"

"Great if you ignore the fact we took off an hour past our departure time, the woman next to me kept burping up beer and someone's kids screamed from the time we took off until we landed. Other than that it couldn't have been more perfect," she said.

"I told you to let me arrange a private flight for you. Noah's wife would have gladly sent one of her planes."

"Noah's wife is very sweet but she doesn't know me from Adam. The woman is running a business, not a personal charity service for the friends of her family."

"Like I won't be repaying her with free meals when she's down here."

Rebecca rolled her eyes skyward. "You're comparing apples and oranges, Nate. Apples and oranges!"

Nathaniel smiled. Rebecca was the only person allowed to shorten his name. Even his twin brother called him by his full name. Rebecca called him Nate and he called her Bec. It was their thing. Others had tried and had been sorely disappointed when corrected. His family often referred to her by her nickname but never called her such to her face, understanding the significance it held for the two of them.

He was still holding on to her and she allowed herself to settle back against his broad chest. The nearness of him had butterflies fluttering in her midsection and her heart racing like a drumline in her chest. She struggled to contain the rise of emotion that had her knees quivering and her legs turning to rubber.

She bent her arms upward to clutch his, her manicured fingers gripping his forearms. He shifted his hips, widening his stance as his body cradled hers. They stood together, still holding on to each other as they stared out over the landscape. The sight of white-capped waves in the distance was intoxicating. The water rolled and rocked against the craggy landscape. The low roar of the waves and the hiss of spray were soothing, pulling them both into deep thought. Neither spoke, not needing words. They settled easily into the comfort they always found when they were with each other. It felt like home and both couldn't have been happier.

From the corner of the building Elise cleared her throat. Nathaniel saw her before Rebecca did. He dropped his arms abruptly and took a step back. "Elise, hey! What brings you here?"

Startled, Rebecca turned. The woman eyeing them curiously didn't look at all pleased. Her teeth were clenched tightly and her cheeks were a vibrant shade of red. She tossed the length of her auburn hair over her shoulders. Rebecca didn't miss how uncomfortable Nathaniel suddenly looked.

Elise cleared her throat and forced a smile to her face. She carried a small potted plant in her hands. "I didn't mean to interrupt. I knew you had a meeting with your contractor and thought I'd stop by to drop off a little housewarming gift of sorts. To congratulate you on closing today." She moved forward, passed the plant to Nathaniel and extended her hand toward Rebecca. "Elise Montgomery. And you are?"

Rebecca forced a smile back. "Rebecca. Rebecca Marks."

Elise looked from her to him and back. "Are you and Nathaniel friends?"

Rebecca smiled. She didn't bother to answer the question, instead turning toward the man who still looked like he'd been caught with his hands in someone's cookie jar. "Why don't I go check out the inside while you deal with your business," she said, her voice dropping an octave. She held out her hand for the keys.

Nathaniel nodded. "Thanks," he said as he watched her move down the side of the building and disappear around the corner. He turned back toward Elise.

"You didn't tell me you were dating someone," Elise sniped.

"Because I'm not dating anyone."

"Well, you and that woman looked quite cozy with each other."

"Elise, you and I are not in a relationship. I really don't owe you any explanations about anything."

Elise took a swift inhale of air and held it for a split second before she responded. "I apologize, Nathaniel.

You know I care about you and I was hoping you and I might be able to move our friendship toward something more. But I don't chase after men who don't want me. If you're not interested, all you had to do was say so."

"I told you the truth, Elise. Right now I'm focused on this restaurant. That's my priority. Everything else will have to take a back seat for a minute. Especially dating and starting a new relationship. I had hoped you would understand that."

"I wasn't trying to make things difficult. I just… well…" She giggled nervously. "I guess I was a little jealous," she said.

He forced himself to smile. Before he could respond, a large man with a lumberjack haircut and full beard called his name, moving swiftly toward them. "Stallion! My man!"

"Carl, hey! It's good to see you," Nathaniel said, moving to shake the other man's hand. "I appreciate you coming."

"I'm excited. This place is spectacular!" Carl said as he looked around, taking in the view. He tilted his head toward Elise. "Hello there. I'm Carl."

"Elise Montgomery, this is Carl Parker. Carl, Elise is my real estate agent," Nathaniel said, making the formal introductions.

"It's very nice to meet you, Carl. I'm surprised we've not met before. Is your business here in Carmel?"

Carl shook his head. "No. My firm is based in Los Angeles. Nathaniel and I are old friends. We met in college when we were pledging the same fraternity. We've been brothers ever since. I actually built his house in LA and when he told me about his plans for this place I jumped at the opportunity to do the renovations he wants."

Nathaniel nodded. "I've got first-rate friends like that," he said.

There was suddenly a knock on the glass windows. The trio turned to look as Rebecca stood inside waving excitedly.

"You didn't tell me our girl was going to be here," Carl exclaimed as he waved back.

Nathaniel grinned. "Who else could do my marketing and promotion?"

"It was nice to meet you, Elise," Carl said. He pointed toward the building. "I'm going to go say hello to Rebecca. Just let me know when you're ready to talk business," he said.

Nathaniel nodded. "I'll be right in."

Elise was still staring at him eagerly, wearing an air of desperation like a beloved perfume. Nathaniel forced a smile onto his face. "Thank you for the plant," he said as he gestured with the potted fern in his hand.

"You're going to call me, right?"

He nodded. "I will. I promise."

Nathaniel watched as Elise threw him one last look over her shoulder. He sighed, a gust of air billowing into the ocean breeze.

Despite his good intentions he instinctively knew Elise would never be in his life the way she hoped to be. Whether it was ever said or not, he would always compare holding a woman in his arms to what it felt like to hold Rebecca. Because just before they'd been interrupted, his holding tight to Rebecca had felt like he'd won the best prize at the state fair.

Chapter 2

When Nathaniel finally made it inside the space that would soon be his new restaurant, Rebecca and Carl were laughing heartily. It had been a good long minute since the two had last seen each other and they were enjoying their moment to catch up.

As he stood watching the two of them it felt like old times. College had brought them into each other's lives. They'd all become fast friends and the bond had continued well after graduation despite the distance and time that had separated them over the years.

Watching Rebecca as she bantered back and forth with Carl made him smile. She'd always been quick with the one-liners. Her sense of humor had often kept them all laughing and she had one of the most infectious smiles. There was something about her that always made him feel that no matter the challenge things would be okay. She had a way of putting him at ease and he trusted her implicitly.

She laughed again, tossing her head back against her shoulders. She was truly stunning, he thought as light danced across her face and joy shimmered in her dark eyes. And she was wearing the hell out of a vibrant green, form-fitting, off-the-shoulder spandex dress that stopped midknee and flattered her chocolate-brown complexion. She wore four-inch heels that accentuated her thick calves and lengthened her long legs even more. She was the epitome of what he and the boys called *thick*. Her breasts were the size of small watermelons, multiple handfuls with spillage and then some. Her childbearing hips and rotund behind were wide and full, like beach balls smooshed tightly together. He thought about the fullness that had pressed comfortably against his groin, the lush cushion that had necessitated some restraint on his part. She'd been abundantly blessed and he had always admired how comfortable she was in her skin.

In college, skinnier women who were starving themselves for what they deemed perfect bodies had found her confidence intimidating. Jealousy had reared its head many times and she'd been the brunt of mean-spirited comments and jokes about her weight. Rebecca hadn't been fazed by any of it. The former high school prom queen, cotillion debutante, choir soloist and Miss California runner-up had clapped back at her critics with a bright smile as she enjoyed every aspect of her existence, living her life to the fullest, unconcerned with what anyone else thought about her. Rebecca was his best friend and he felt immensely blessed that she still gave him the time of day.

Rebecca calling his name pulled him from the reflections he'd fallen into. He looked up to find her staring at him, her hands clutching her waistline, her hips pushed to one side. Her thick, jet-black hair hung to her midback, lush waves with the slightest hint of curl. He smiled as she tossed a few stray strands over her shoulder.

"I want it known, for the record, that Carl doesn't like your new girlfriend."

Carl laughed and choked at the same time. He held up an open hand. "I did not say that!"

Nathaniel shook his head. "Elise is not my girlfriend."

"I couldn't tell with the way she started interrogating me," Rebecca said, her brow raised slightly.

Nathaniel's grin was wide, a deep crevice in the center of his face highlighting his perfect white teeth and the dimples in his cheeks. "She asked you one question, Bec. You're being a little dramatic."

"Me? Dramatic?" Rebecca crossed her arms over her chest. "I am never dramatic!"

"I know that's a lie," Nathaniel quipped. He moved toward the bar and took a seat.

"Carl also said she looks like a poodle that's been wound up too tight. That pinched face was not cute!"

The other man was still laughing heartily. He shook his head, his hands waving back and forth as he tried to catch his breath.

Nathaniel chuckled. "He did not. I know you, Bec."

She moved to where he sat and pulled up the stool beside him. "So, really, what's up with you and Susie Homemaker."

"Nothing. Yet. She helped me find this place and we've talked about maybe hanging out together after I get the restaurant open. It's nothing serious though."

"You and your women never are," Rebecca teased.

Nathaniel shrugged. "This could be different. You never now. It's about time I thought about settling down. Right?"

Carl shook his head. "You really don't want to do that. Trust me," he said. "Marriage isn't everything it's cracked up to be."

"Says the man who is on his fourth wife!" Rebecca said with a laugh.

"Angel is my third wife, thank you very much. Lisa or Terry might be my fourth wife. Not quite sure yet."

Rebecca rolled her eyes skyward. "You are such a man!"

"And you are seriously making us all look bad," Nathaniel interjected.

The trio laughed, falling back into their easy way of being with each other. Despite how long it had been since they were last together it was like old times all over again. After a few minutes catching up, Nathaniel and Carl moved to take a tour of the building so that

Nathaniel could point out the changes and renovations he wanted done fast and quick.

Rebecca stared after him. Everything about Nathaniel Stallion made her heart skip beats. Nathaniel had always been a man who dazzled without even knowing that he had that kind of swag. In school, he'd been the studious type, focused on his grades and his future. His twin brother Nicholas had garnered the attention on and off the football field. Nathaniel had been the serious brother, not nearly as outgoing and a little slow for the lengthy list of females enamored with his dark eyes.

He had an athletic build, his body a strong, solid mass of rock-hard muscle. Regular workouts kept him in fit shape. He was tall, with legs like solid tree trunks and a café au lait complexion that was as much coffee as it was cream. She watched as he scaled a ladder. He wore denim jeans and the view from where she sat was quite delectable. She bit down against her bottom lip to stall the quiver of heat that suddenly pierced her feminine spirit.

Wanting Nathaniel from a distance was one thing. Wanting him when he was close enough to reach out and touch was something else. For a split second Rebecca found herself questioning whether or not coming to help had been a smart decision. And then she thought about the other woman who clearly had her sights set on something happening between her and Nathaniel. He had said *yet*. Which meant he was actually considering the prospect of something happening with him and his new buddy Elise. The thought made Rebecca cringe with irritation and envy.

She blew a soft sigh. Nathaniel was much more than just her best friend. She couldn't imagine her life without him and she always feared that a serious relationship with another woman might be the end of the bond they shared. She loved him and she knew he cared about her just as deeply. But Nathaniel had never looked at her as anything more than a friend. And as she thought about it, Rebecca realized, she had never before given him any reason to see her any differently.

"So have you finally decided on the name yet?" Rebecca sat on Nathaniel's family room sofa, watching as he moved about casually in his kitchen.

"The name?"

"For the restaurant. What do you plan to call it? I know there were two at the top of your list that you really liked. Which one did you decide on?"

Nathaniel lifted his gaze to stare at her. Her hair was pulled into a high ponytail and her feet were bare. She had changed into a T-shirt and sweatpants and looked quite comfortable where she rested, her legs extended atop the ottoman. A playlist of soft jazz and blues billowed through the air, painting the walls with a bold hint of chill.

The afternoon had gone longer than either had anticipated. The list of things needed to meet his deadline with the restaurant had gotten more and more extensive as they and Carl had brainstormed together. Most of the work Carl needed to do was cosmetic: minor wood-work repairs and paint. Only one major wall needed to be blown out to open the dining room and both the men's and women's bathrooms would be gutted and completely replaced with new fixtures and tile. There was also the installation of the stage and dance floor that he'd insisted on. With the exception of a few appliances already scheduled to be replaced the kitchen was top-notch.

Staffing was being handled by an outside agency, and the list of potential employees ready to be interviewed had exploded hours after their advertisement had hit the local newspaper. Rebecca had already begun the marketing and promotional plan, starting with the setup of the website and social media pages.

"I need the business name, Nate."

"Dinner."

"Excuse me?"

"*Dinner.* I'm calling the restaurant Dinner."

There was a moment of pause as Rebecca reflected on his comment. She muttered softly under her breath. "Thank you for calling Dinner. Welcome to Dinner. Let's go to Dinner for dinner!" She jotted notes into the lined pad on her lap. Her voice rose an octave. "Why did you choose Dinner? Why not The Melting Pot or one of the others?"

"Dinner just felt right. When you think about the menu and the ambience the restaurant will have, it just works." He stepped into the room, swiping his hands against a dishcloth. "Why? Don't you like it?"

"Actually, I think it's perfect. And I had a feeling, after our last conversation, that it was the one you were leaning toward which is why I had my team do some mockups of the logos and signage. I think you're going to be pretty pleased." She gestured with a file folder of documents that she'd pulled from the leather attaché at the foot of the chair.

Nathaniel moved to her side, dropping down onto the sofa beside her. He took the folder from her hands and began to flip through its contents. As he studied the documents inside, a wave of emotion suddenly consumed him. It was rife with exhilaration and a hint of anxiety. A single, solitary tear rolled past his lashes.

"Is everything okay?" Rebecca asked, her tone consoling. "Are they that bad?"

He chuckled, shaking his head. "Actually, they're that good. I'm very impressed."

"Is that's why you're all teary?"

"I'm not teary, Bec!"

"Could have fooled me," she said, her warm smile encouraging his. She knew him and knew something was on his mind. Something needing to be said.

Nathaniel spun his body lengthwise and rested his head in her lap. He settled himself comfortably against her as he flipped through the folder a second time. "I really like this second set. It's perfect."

Rebecca nodded. "That's my favorite, too. It's bold yet the edges are just soft enough. It's inviting. And it looks amazing on the menu!"

Nathaniel shifted his eyes upward to stare at her.

He let the folder fall down against his abdomen. He heaved a deep breath and then a second as he seemed to be gathering his thoughts and searching for the right words. Rebecca let him ponder the moment and waited patiently for him to say what was bothering him.

"This is really happening, Bec," he said finally, an air of awe in his tone. "It's been five years since I first thought about doing this and now it's really about to happen."

"It is, and it's going to be a major success. You've already had five years to work out the kinks."

Nathaniel chuckled. "I can only hope it'll be that easy."

"Look, you have plotted every possible scenario of what could go wrong. You have laid the groundwork for contingency plans B, C and D, if A doesn't work out. You've got this."

"I couldn't have done it without you."

"I know," Bec said as she brushed her index finger across his brow.

Nathaniel suddenly lifted himself upright, spinning his feet back to the floor. "Do we need to bring in your luggage?"

"I dropped my stuff off at the hotel earlier."

"The hotel?"

Rebecca nodded. "I've got a room at the La Playa while I'm here."

"So, how did you change clothes?" he asked, confusion washing over his expression.

"You know I always keep something with me, just

in case. I always carry a change of clothes in the gym bag that I keep with me."

"Just in case what?"

"In case I meet someone and need to make a quick change," she said sarcastically.

Nathaniel shook his head. "You didn't need to get a hotel. You know you can stay here. I have two guest bedrooms."

"I can't stay here."

"Yes, you can. You know you're always welcome."

"I do know that. But I can't stay here."

"Why not?"

"I can't."

"You're being ridiculous, Bec."

"Maybe I am, Nate, but I'm still staying at the hotel."

The two sat staring at each other. Rebecca wished she could explain and have it make sense. She knew if she tried, it would only make the moment more awkward between them. She also knew that deep down Nathaniel probably didn't want an explanation, both grateful they wouldn't have to go through the rituals friends do when they intrude on each other's private spaces. She changed the subject.

"So tell me about this woman."

"Who? Elise?"

"Don't play dumb. You know exactly who I'm talking about."

He rolled his eyes. "There's nothing to tell. Not really."

"Did she help you find this place too?"

Nathaniel shook his head. "No. One of my fraternity brothers owns the agency she works for. He helped find me the house. She just happened to be the listing agent for the restaurant."

"Do you like her?"

Nathaniel shifted his gaze back to hers to stare. Rebecca was eyeing him intently, eager for him to respond. He shrugged his shoulders. "I don't really know her."

"Are you trying to know her?"

"Not at the moment. I'm focused on my business and that's all."

There was a moment of silence as she pondered his response. He broke the silence.

"Are you still dating that Michael guy?"

"His name is Maxwell."

"Yeah. Whatever. You two still an item?"

"We were never an item. We went out a few times then it got weird."

"Weird how?"

"Just when I was thinking about taking things to the next level he started acting strangely."

"What do you mean?"

She snatched her eyes from his, her stare skipping around the room. "It was embarrassing, actually."

Nathaniel shifted himself around to stare at her. "Okay, spill it. What did he do and why is this the first time I'm hearing about it?"

"I don't tell you everything, Nate."

"That's your first mistake," he said matter-of-factly.

"Had you asked for help I might have been able to save your relationship."

Rebecca laughed. "Who said I wanted to save it?"

He eyed her with a raised brow. "So what did what's-his-name do?"

"When we talked about having sex, he asked me if I would be willing to wear a strap-on dildo and peg him."

"I don't even know what that means but it doesn't even sound kosher."

"You know what pegging is, *Doctor* Stallion."

"Like hell I do! Educate me, please."

She shook her head in disbelief. "He wanted me to wear a rubber dick to penetrate him anally. That's pegging."

Nathaniel blinked his eyes, his lashes batting rapidly. He suddenly burst out laughing. "Well! I can see your problem with that."

A smirk crossed Rebecca's face "Thank you."

"But your first mistake was talking about having sex. If you need to make it a discussion, he's not the guy for you. And it's the first time, too? You're too spontaneous for that. If he was the right guy it would have come to you naturally."

"So, you don't discuss sex with your partners before you have sex?"

"Of course, I do. It's important to know what my woman likes so that I can please her."

"But you don't talk about it before you do it? You don't discuss possible consequences, expectations, nothing?"

"I talk about where she wants me to put my tongue."

"You are such a pervert!"

Nathaniel laughed as Rebecca changed the subject. "It was really great catching up with Carl. I missed him."

"You two live less than an hour from each other. It doesn't make sense that your paths never cross."

Rebecca shrugged. "Things have always been a little weird with us since he made that pass at me."

"Was that before wife number two or after? I can't remember."

"After. He was engaged to wife number three when it happened."

"In his defense he was plastered. I don't think he's drunk that much since."

"That's no defense."

Nathaniel shrugged, his broad shoulders reaching for the ceiling. "You just need to do a better job keeping up with your friends. And that includes me."

"I talk to you every day."

"Yeah, but when I'm in LA, I rarely see you."

"Do you ever stop complaining?" Rebecca's eyes were wide, a hint of annoyance painting her expression.

Nathaniel laughed. "I wasn't complaining. I was just pointing out a fact."

Before either realized it, they had talked most of the night away. It was well past midnight when Rebecca twice moved to leave. Then the conversation would change again, and again, another hour passed them by.

Nathaniel didn't know who fell asleep first, only that when he woke, the sun was just beginning to rise outside his windows and Rebecca was snoring softly beside him.

He knew she wasn't going to be happy that she'd never made it to the hotel. She complained just as much as she accused him of doing. But both only complained to each other, something about misery loving company. The thought made him smile.

He still didn't understand why she insisted on a hotel room when he had more than enough space for her to stay. He'd been in the house for almost a year, the purchase originally intended to be a vacation home from the demands his medical practice had made on him. The 2600-square-foot home had been built in the late twenties. The stone exterior, wood paneling and rock-faced fireplaces gave the space an old-world appearance and feel. One side of the property was surrounded by majestic cypress trees. The other spotlighted the sights and sounds of the Pacific. The house was situated on less than an acre of land that showcased the spectacular ocean views he'd come to love and with the open entertainment areas, three large bedrooms and bathrooms, and the renovated chef's kitchen, it was quickly becoming his primary residence. As far as he was concerned, there were more reasons for Bec to stay than not to stay.

He sat upright, easing himself from her. She shifted against the sofa cushions, rolling over to curl her body around one of the oversized pillows. Two deep breaths and she resumed her low snore without missing a beat.

The sound both amused and soothed him. Staring down at her he resisted the urge to trail his hand over her luscious hips and backside. Eyeing the delectable curves moved the muscle between his legs to tighten and he inhaled swiftly to stall the twitch of nature that threatened to bloom into a full-fledged morning erection.

Rising from the sofa he moved swiftly toward the master bathroom and the oversized shower. He stripped out of his clothes as he entered the bedroom, leaving a trail of garments on the floor behind him. Seconds later he stood under the spray of hot water, releasing the tension that tightened his shoulders and the last remnants of grogginess wanting to pull him back to sleep. In his head he ran through his lengthy to-do list, trying to determine when or if he'd be able to squeeze in a run and time in the gym with the weight machines.

Nathaniel lost track of time. When he finally stepped out of the shower, refreshed and invigorated, it could have been a few minutes or a good hour that had passed. He only knew he needed to get down to the restaurant to meet with his new suppliers. He dressed quickly and moved back to the living space.

As he moved down the short length of hallway he called Rebecca's name. When she didn't answer he shook his head. He didn't need to look to know that his best friend was gone. A note scribbled on lined paper rested where she'd laid her head. The print was neat and bold, her handwriting familiar in her favorite green ink. A few quick lines promised that she'd catch up with him sometime during the day. She too had work to do.

Chapter 3

Freshly showered, Rebecca sat buck naked in the center of the hotel's king-sized bed with her laptop, her iPad and two cell phones. Technology had made conducting her business behind the privacy of a closed door a luxury she had no intentions of ever losing. Being her own boss allowed her perks a regular nine-to-five job didn't afford.

She scrolled through her list of things to do, ticking off the last few items for the day. Signage, menus and paper products had been ordered for Nathaniel's restaurant. He'd approved the final logo and designs and with the many pieces needed for him to open falling into place, his excitement fueled hers.

Carl and his crew were already knee-deep in the

renovations and they were only two short weeks from the tables and chairs being delivered. Both she and Nathaniel had pulled every favor ever owed to them to make everything happen as quickly as it needed to. Rebecca had snapped her fingers, cajoled and coddled egos, and had begged and prayed in order to help her friend achieve his goals. Others would have balked at the challenge. She'd embraced it. For him.

She knew from his text messages that he wasn't too thrilled about her walking out without at least saying goodbye first. But she knew he'd get over it and forgive her that small slight. When she'd woken and found him in the shower she'd resisted the urge to strip out of her clothes and join him. Slipping out of the door like a thief on a mission had been her only option. Because everything in her had just wanted to strip off her clothes.

Her cell phone chimed, interrupting the memory. She bit down against her bottom lip to stall the quiver of heat that pulsed for attention, focusing instead on the call.

Felicia Marks began to rant the minute Rebecca said hello.

"I have been calling you since you took off without telling anyone where you were going. Have you completely lost your mind?" Rebecca's older sister admonished.

"I left you a message."

"*Be back in a few weeks.* That's what your message said. That's all your message said. *Be back in a few weeks.* Not where you were disappearing to. Not if you were with someone. Not what your plans were. Not how many weeks was a few. Your note said nothing. And then you stopped answering your cell phone!"

"But I left one!" Rebecca said, her singsong tone meant to annoy her oldest sibling even more. She sensed her sister shaking her head on the other end of the phone and imagined the glare painting the woman's expression.

"You are so lucky that I can't get my hands on you right now."

"You worry too much. I'm perfectly fine."

"Where are you?"

"Carmel-by-the-Sea. With Nathaniel Stallion. Helping him to open his new restaurant. I think I told you about it when he first mentioned the idea."

"Really, Rebecca? I know you do not expect me to believe that you just snuck off without telling anyone just to continue pretending you're not in love with that man. Restaurant my behind!"

"Nathaniel and I are just friends. That's all."

"So who's handling your other clients while you're away?"

"I do have employees and I can work from wherever. Technology has come a long way since your DOS-based computer programs and HP calculators. We use the internet now. You should give it a try," she said facetiously.

"Don't be a wise-ass, Rebecca. I'm concerned about you."

"You shouldn't, sissy. I'm a big girl and I know what I'm doing."

"Are you ever going to tell him, Rebecca?"

"Right now I am going to get dressed and go take a walk along the beach. It's been a long and productive day and I deserve to treat myself. That is what I'm going to do. I might even buy myself some ice cream."

"Here is where I'd give you my lecture about not being afraid to take risks and how you should step out on faith and trust in what fate has in store for you. Because you are so in love with that man! You should tell him, Rebecca. But since I know you'll ignore me and pretend you don't have a clue what I'm talking about, I won't waste my breath. I'll just tell him myself the next time I see the two of you."

"You wouldn't dare!" Rebecca quipped.

Felicia laughed. "Wouldn't I?"

"I am so done with you right now. Are we good? Are you satisfied that I'm still alive and breathing so you can go back to whatever it is you do?"

"Call me tomorrow, Rebecca, or I will call you."

"Bye, Felicia!"

"That really isn't cute anymore," Felicia laughed. "It's not cute at all!"

Rebecca disconnected the line. She waited a quick second and then she sent her sister a text message, simply saying, I love you.

She dropped into reflection, thinking about her situation. Rebecca knew she didn't always make it easy for the people who cared about her. Her sister Felicia and Nathaniel especially. It was bad enough that she still had to explain her disappearing act to him but she didn't have the energy to also explain herself to her sister. Especially since her sister knew her so well. Felicia read her as easily as Nathaniel did, and Rebecca didn't always need to say things out loud.

Her sister was her best female friend. Most times they were like oil and water, Felicia holding her up while she floated all willy-nilly in the atmosphere. It had been that way since they'd been little girls. She had only told Felicia what she felt for Nathaniel and that was after way too many alcoholic beverages. The two had been on a girl's weekend bender, determined to have a good time while still managing to stay out of trouble. She'd let her secret spill and Felicia had been giving her a hard time ever since. But the more she thought about it, the more she was starting to think that maybe her sister was right. Maybe it was time to tell Nathaniel how she felt, to expose her hand and hope he was open to the possibilities.

Another message chimed on the device in her hand. She had lost count of the number of messages Nathaniel had sent to get her attention. She hadn't lost sight of the fact she'd ignored most of them. She stole a quick glance to the digital clock on the nightstand. She'd missed lunch and the biscuit she'd eaten for breakfast was a distant memory. She was hungry and finally texted him back about when and where.

She could do dinner, she thought, beginning to gather her belongings from the bed. And because she knew he would have questions, she began to prep her answers, getting her excuses and story in order.

* * *

Nathaniel's brow was raised, his eyes wide, as he stared at her. The two were seated at Bar Mars, a popular dinner spot that catered to a wealthy crowd of pretty people. Rebecca had insisted he check out his competition, wanting to critique the food and the ambience. After one size-thin woman too many had vied for his attention as if Rebecca weren't standing by his side, she'd been having second thoughts about them coming there. She took a deep breath and held it, knowing he expected an answer to his question. He repeated himself.

"I'm serious, Bec. I really want to know why you left the way you did. And why you won't just stay at the house."

She rolled her eyes skyward. "It really isn't a big deal, Nate. We both had things to do. You were in the shower and I needed one. It just made sense for me to go back to the hotel where my things were."

Nathaniel shook his head. "Then you ignore my calls all day. I was starting to think I'd done something to offend you."

"You know how I am," Rebecca said. "I just needed some time to myself."

"I would have thought you'd outgrown those mood swings by now," he said with a wry grin.

She laughed. "Nope and I'm still prone to throwing tantrums when I can't have my way. You've been warned."

Nathaniel nodded. "My invitation still stands," he said. "There is more than enough room at the house for you and your stuff. You don't need to stay at that hotel." He reached into his pocket and pulled out a single key on a silver key ring, passing it to her.

"What is this?"

"It's the key to my house. You use it to unlock the doors."

Rebecca closed her eyes and took another deep breath. When she opened them, the look he was giving her caused a ripple of heat to trail down the length of her spine. She clenched her fists tightly together. "You're giving me the keys to your house?"

"Why wouldn't I? It just makes sense that you should be able to come and go as you please."

"I am not going to just let myself into your home like I live there. Not going to happen!"

"Why are you always so damn stubborn?"

"Me? What about you? Always trying to tell people what to do."

He grinned. "I just tell you what to do and you never listen to me."

"I'm still not staying at your house or using a key."

Nathaniel nodded. "Yes, you will!" And then he reached across the table and dropped the keyring into her purse.

Rebecca was ready with a snarky response when someone suddenly called her name. She and Nathaniel both turned at the same time, gazes shifting toward the deep baritone voice with the familiar Caribbean lilt.

"Rebecca Marks! I thought that was you!"

Rebecca's eyes widened as she fixated on the man

moving swiftly in her direction. She stole the quickest glance toward Nathaniel who was eyeing them both curiously.

"Is that who I think it is?" he muttered under his breath.

Rebecca mumbled back. "Yep! That's my former fiancé."

As the man reached their table, Rebecca forced a smile to her face. "Jeffrey Baylor! What a surprise!" she gushed, moving onto the platform heels she'd worn.

Jeffrey swept her into his arms and spun her in a circle. His excitement was palpable, the wealth of it making it seem like it had taken over the room. Those at the tables closest to them turned to stare, smiles widening as the two old friends greeted each other. When the man suddenly kissed her, pressing his mouth tightly to hers, Nathaniel felt himself bristle with indignation, a flagrant wave of jealousy sweeping through him. He was on his feet before he realized it, his stance just aggressive enough to pull at Rebecca's attention.

She swiped the back of her hand across her full lips, her face tinged a brilliant shade of deep red. "Jeffrey, you remember Nathaniel Stallion, don't you? He went to school with us," she said as she took a step back, pulling herself from the man's clutches.

"How could I forget. It's good to see you, Stallion."

"It's good to see you as well," Nathaniel said, his tone dry. "What a small world."

"Not small enough," Jeffrey quipped with a slight chuckle. He turned his full focus back on Rebecca.

"You are as beautiful as ever, Rebecca! So what are you doing here?"

Rebecca smiled. "Working," she said, taking another quick glance toward Nathaniel. "Nathaniel is opening a restaurant not too far from here, so we thought we should come check out the competition."

Jeffrey nodded, a smile pulling at his mouth. "I'm flattered that you see me and my restaurant as competition."

Rebecca and Nathaniel both looked stunned. "You own this place?" Nathaniel questioned.

"I do. Five years now."

"So, you did put those culinary skills of yours to good use! We're very impressed."

"We're not that impressed," Nathaniel muttered under his breath.

Rebecca's laugh was a nervous titter. She was suddenly hypersensitive, her emotions on serious overload. She inhaled swiftly and held the warm breath deep in her lungs.

As third wheels go, Jeffrey didn't appear to notice her discomfort and didn't seem to care much about Nathaniel's. He gestured for them both to retake their seats and then slid into the booth with them, into the empty space beside Rebecca. He eyed Nathaniel intently.

"So, Stallion, you purchased the restaurant property on Mile Drive. I'd put a bid in on it, but obviously I lost out. Although, I have to say I think you paid way too much for it!"

Nathaniel snorted. "It's an investment I'll easily recoup."

"I'm sure you know the restaurant business isn't an easy one. But I wish you luck with yours."

"Nathaniel will do very well. We're very excited for what his restaurant will bring to the area," Rebecca interjected, sounding very much like a marketing professional. She and Nathaniel exchanged a look, he eyeing her with a raised brow.

Jeffry dropped a hand to her thigh and she tensed, his touch causing her breath to hitch. She pulled away from his grasp, shifting herself closer to the wall. The man smiled and winked an eye at her. "It's great that you have such talent working for you," he said, shifting his gaze back toward Nathaniel. "Now, correct me if I'm wrong, Stallion, but weren't you planning on a medical career when we were in school?"

"Actually, it's Dr. Stallion and I've had a very successful surgical career since graduation and med school."

"So the restaurant is just an investment thing for you?"

Rebecca chimed in a second time. "Not at all. Nathaniel is deeply committed to this new venture. He will be very hands-on with the day-to-day operations. He's a marvelous chef and has gotten rave reviews for the two pop-up restaurants he tested in Los Angeles last year."

Jeffry smiled. "Well, I look forward to visiting your place when you get it open, Stallion." He stood back up. "Rebecca, I'd love to catch up. Maybe we can grab coffee one day this week? That is if you can tear yourself away from your *work* for a short while."

Rebecca smiled. "Maybe."

He pulled a ballpoint pen and a business card from the breast pocket of his button-down shirt. He jotted a phone number on the back then winked his eye at her a second time. "Here's my number. Please. Call me. I'd love for us to sit down and talk."

Rebecca nodded, her face lifting in a sweet smile. "I will do that," she responded.

Nathaniel met Jeffrey's outstretched hand with his own and shook it. "It was good seeing you again, Jeff," he said politely.

The two watched as Jeffrey took his leave, sauntering back across the room and through the swinging doors into the employees-only area.

"Well, that was a surprise," Rebecca quipped as casually as she could muster.

Nathaniel sensed her feeling out his mood as she tried to make sense of her own emotions. He nodded. "It's not often you run into your ex-fiancé. Must have been like old times the way he was so touchy-feely."

"It was not like that."

"You sure about that, Bec? You looked like you were enjoying his attention."

"I did not!"

"You did, too! And that's okay if you were. I know how much you loved him. You were ready to throw your whole life away to follow him around the world. The way it ended left a lot unsaid. You may still have some residual feelings for him."

Rebecca closed her eyes. Jeffrey Baylor had been so lost in her past that she had never imagined ever having to revisit him or that time period again. He'd arrived as a transfer student at UCLA their junior year. Tall, dark and handsome to the nth degree, he'd captured the attention of every woman on campus and Rebecca had captured his. His pursuit of her had been taken right out of the handbook for a romance novel. He'd said and done all the right things, never amiss with the romantic attention. He'd had her swooning by the third date and before she knew it she'd been his girl. Even then Nathaniel's teasing her about it had been unmerciful.

But her best friend and her boyfriend had never meshed, unable to find any common ground. Not even her happiness. The two had butted heads at every turn, like two bulls in a china shop racing for the door. Nathaniel hadn't trusted the man and had often pointed out flaws she'd chosen to ignore. When her grades slipped, her attention divided, he'd blamed her love life, often admonishing her to get back on track.

Jeffrey had graduated the year before she and Nathaniel did, with plans to head to France for a culinary career. When he'd shown up on her doorstep begging her to join him, she had wanted to say yes. When Nathaniel found out, enumerating every reason why that was a bad idea, doubt had set in. Although the two had never discussed it, the words never said out loud, she and Jeffrey had known that if she'd been made to choose one over the other, Nathaniel would have always won. He'd known and he had hated it and despised Nathaniel for it. But Nathaniel owned her heart, Jeffrey had only occupied a very small piece of it. She could have loved Jeffrey but she would have always been *in love* with Nathaniel. It had been the difference between her leaving and her final decision to stay. And Nathaniel didn't have a clue.

She opened her eyes to stare at her friend. "You really don't know what the hell you're talking about, Nate."

"I know what I see, Bec."

"Do you really? I swear, you are such a jerk sometimes!" she hissed between clenched teeth. She stood up abruptly.

"Where are you going?"

"Back to my hotel room."

"I thought you wanted to go walk on the beach?"

"You just ruined the mood!" she said and with a dismissive flick of her hand and a twirl on her high heels she stomped toward the door and out of the restaurant.

Chapter 4

Nathaniel hated when Rebecca was angry with him. It had been three days since she'd stormed out of the restaurant, pissed beyond measure. He still didn't have a clue why she'd gotten so furious or how he could fix what he'd apparently broken. His calls weren't being answered and his business dealings had been passed on to one of her associates. If he hadn't checked, he wouldn't have even known if she were still registered at the hotel.

He was barely listening to Naomi and Natalie who were both chattering away on the three-way call. When one of them, and he wasn't sure which, called his name, pulling at his attention, he was genuinely surprised.

"Are you still on the line?" Naomi snapped.

"Yeah! I'm here. What's wrong?" he questioned.

"We should be asking you that," Natalie said. "You haven't heard a word either of us has said for the last ten minutes. What's wrong with you?"

"And we want the truth," Naomi added.

Nathaniel heaved a deep sigh. "I just have a lot on my mind. Getting this restaurant open is just a challenge, that's all."

"And how is Rebecca?" Naomi asked, not bothering to beat around the bush.

"She is still working on the restaurant with you, right?"

"Does anything get past you two?" Nathaniel asked.

Both women answered simultaneously. "No!"

He chuckled softly. "She's got an attitude about something and she's not talking to me."

"What did you do?" Natalie quipped.

"And why haven't you fixed it?" Naomi interjected.

"Why is this my fault? I didn't do anything. She's just crazy! I'm sure all of it has something to do with that ex-boyfriend of hers. We ran into him at dinner the other night. He owns a restaurant not far from mine."

"So did something happen to upset her?"

Nathaniel spent the next few minutes filling them in on the minor details of his time with Rebecca. He concluded, "Then she blew up when I told her I thought she still had feelings for him. But you should have seen how she was when he was hugging her all up. And he even kissed her! Clearly, she didn't seem to mind that, right?"

Naomi laughed, noting the agitation in her brother's

tone. "When are you and Rebecca going to stop playing this game with each other?"

"What game?"

"Pretending you don't have feelings for each other," Natalie quipped.

"It's not like that. We're great friends and I care about her, but…"

"You love her, big brother. You've always loved her. You've just been afraid to admit it," Naomi said, adding her two cents to the conversation.

"I'm not saying I don't love Bec, I'm saying…"

"That you are a complete and total moron!" Natalie said. "You are such a man it makes my jaw tight!"

"What? I am not that bad."

"You're worse. You're so busy telling Rebecca what you see between her and some other guy, but you're blind to what's happening right up under your nose with you and her."

"I'm not blind. I…well…it's complicated," he said finally.

"So do you want us to tell you how to fix it?" Naomi asked.

Nathaniel hesitated. When he finally said, "Yes," the two sisters laughed warmly.

"Start with flowers and an apology," Natalie said.

"Definitely flowers," Naomi cosigned. "Rebecca is very much a romantic. You're going to have to pursue her. Flowers, candy and romantic dinners to start with."

"And that's only going to get her talking to you

again. If you really want to take your relationship further, you're going to have to get very creative."

"Very creative. Noah is much better at that than you are so you might want to call him for some ideas when you get to that point."

"I know how to be creative," Nathaniel said.

"Says no woman you've ever dated!" Natalie laughed.

"I'm done with this conversation," he finally said. "You two are about to drive me crazy."

"Just keep us posted," Natalie said.

"We're here if you need us," Naomi cosigned.

"I actually think we should call Rebecca, too. Feel her out for him."

"You're right," Naomi agreed, the two women slipping into a conversation that didn't include him.

"You know he's going to mess it up, right?"

"Yes. But we really need to give him more credit than that. He might figure it out."

"I cannot believe you girls," Nathaniel interjected. "I'm hanging up now and do not…I repeat…do not call Rebecca. I will kill you both if you do."

The sisters laughed, their voices echoing over the line at the same time. "We love you, too, Nathaniel!"

Nathaniel started with flowers. Beautiful bouquets of yellow roses. When the first few dozen arrived, Rebecca had been moved to tears. As they kept coming, her hotel suite beginning to look like it had been attacked by a flower fairy, she knew she couldn't avoid him a minute longer. She was just about to dial his phone when there was another knock on the hotel room door. There had been a steady stream of hotel employees delivering the arrangements and anticipating another was just about to send her back into a foul mood. She pushed the number to connect her line to his and pulled the phone to her ear. She threw the door to her room open at the same time.

The cell phone in Nathaniel's pocket vibrated just as Rebecca opened the door. He juggled the large vase in his arms as he reached for the device. "Hey," he said, "Sorry, but I need to answer..."

She shook her head. "It's only me," she said, waving her own phone in her hand.

She pushed the call-end button and his cell phone stopped vibrating. "Hey."

Nathaniel smiled. "May I come in?"

Rebecca took a step back and gestured with her hand for him to pass. As he did, the aroma of his cologne mingled sweetly with the scent of roses, teasing her senses. She inhaled him, biting down against her bottom lip to stall the rise of desire that threatened to interrupt the moment. Nathaniel gave her a brilliantly white smile as he handed her the bouquet of roses he'd been holding. Once inside he turned to face her and watched as she set the flowers onto a table.

"Thank you for the flowers. They're absolutely beautiful, but how many roses did you order?" Rebecca asked.

Nathaniel shrugged his shoulders. "A few."

Rebecca laughed. "You're crazy, you do know that right?"

"I can't have you mad at me, Bec," he said. "It throws me off my game when you're mad at me."

"I'm sorry."

Nathaniel was suddenly at a loss for words. He'd been expecting an argument so when Rebecca apologized, it was unexpected and surprising. She repeated herself as he stood with his mouth open, studying her intently.

"I really owe you an apology for my bad behavior."

He nodded. "Yes, you do," he finally said, pushing his chest out ever so slightly. "I didn't do anything to deserve you treating me like you did, Bec."

She shifted her weight to one hip, her head tilting as she narrowed her gaze. Her index finger waved from side to side. "Don't push your luck, Nate. I'm willing to take responsibility for my actions but you don't get off that easily for what you did."

He tossed up his hands. "Please! Tell me what it was I did. Because I don't have a clue."

She swept past him and took a seat on the sofa. She gestured for him to sit in the wingchair across from her, then shifted forward so she could eye him evenly.

As he sat down Nathaniel found himself drawn to the hint of cleavage that peeked past the opening of her blouse and the curve of her hips nestled against the sofa's cushions. The look that suddenly swept between them was filled with emotion neither had anticipated. It was heated and teasing and promised something wholeheartedly decadent.

Rebecca forced herself to shake the sensation away

before she spoke. "I don't really do a good job communicating with you. Your sisters helped me to see that."

"They actually called you?"

She smiled. "They wanted to check on me. They said they had talked to you already."

"I'm going to kill them both. I just want you to know that it's going to be premeditated and painful. I am so embarrassed! I have no doubts that I probably owe you an apology now."

Rebecca laughed. "I like your sisters. And they were just concerned about you. Natalie said she even thought you might have been crying about the situation."

"I definitely wasn't crying, Bec."

Rebecca shrugged. "We just need to do a better job talking to each other. And I promise to tell you when I'm upset about something instead of holding it in and then blowing up over it."

"Well, since we're going to be all open and honest about things, you hurt my feelings, Bec. We've always been able to talk about everything and suddenly that was a problem."

"That wasn't the problem. The problem was you making assumptions and accusing me of things that weren't true."

"You mean about your boyfriend Jeffrey?"

"He is not my boyfriend!" she snapped, an air of exasperation in her tone.

Nathaniel held up his hands as if he were surrendering. "Sorry, I was just teasing. You don't have to get all sensitive about it."

"Yes. I do. This isn't college and we're not kids anymore. I took a lot of flak from you when we were in school over Jeffrey. I shouldn't have to do it now. You're my best friend. Hell, after my sister, you're probably my only friend! If I cared anything at all about that fool, you know you'd be the first person I would tell. Because I can tell you almost everything."

"Only almost?"

She hesitated. "Everything important."

Nathaniel took a deep breath. "I'm sorry. Clearly, we had a misunderstanding. But when I saw Jeffrey it had me feeling some kind of way. I've never liked that guy and I didn't appreciate the way he thought he could just manhandle you like it was old times."

"You act like I can't handle myself with Jeffrey."

"No other man has ever had the kind of effect on you that Jeffrey Baylor has always had."

"You don't know that."

"I think I do."

"And I'm telling you that you don't. And if you are truly my friend and you care about me the way you say you do then you need to trust that I know what I'm talking about when I tell you something"

He nodded. "You're right. I should never have accused you of still being in love with Jeffrey. You've told me many times that you didn't have feelings like that for him and I should have believed you. But you know I love you, right? You're my very best friend, Bec. That's why I only want what's best for you!"

A tear threatened to fall past her thick lashes. "I love

you, too," she said. "Which is why we both need to do better with each other."

"So can we please hug it out now?" Nathaniel asked as he stood up, his arms outstretched.

Rebecca smiled as she stood and walked into them. She looped her arms around his waist and settled her face against his chest. Her eyes closed as he nestled his face into her hair, drawing her even closer to him. Everything in both their worlds suddenly felt okay again.

Rebecca directed teams of people in the restaurant. The space was beginning to take shape and it was requiring excessive amounts of time from her and Nathaniel. She gave orders like she was discussing the beautiful weather, calm and easy, with her to-do list lengthy and continually growing. She gave Carl direction when she was unhappy with the color of the wood stain. She gave Nathaniel and the new chef orders when she wasn't happy about the desserts. She told the new hostess and the wait staff who were training what she liked or didn't. She stepped up when Nathaniel least expected and he found himself enjoying the team effort between them. She was as invested in his dream as he was.

Their day had been exceptionally long as the tables and chairs had been delivered and installed. When they'd walked out, locking the doors for the night, the restaurant actually looked like a restaurant. He'd been overjoyed and Rebecca had found a problem with the tile flooring. Nathaniel chuckled softly to himself as he thought about it all.

He stirred cinnamon and nutmeg into the orange glaze that simmered on his stovetop. The sweet aroma of sugar and spices scented the air. He had promised Rebecca he would make her favorite foods at least once and he was being true to his word. The menu was a garlic-infused pork shoulder that he'd been smoking over a cherry wood fire for most of the afternoon. He planned to pair it with candied yams seasoned with brown sugar, sautéed mixed greens and freshly baked rolls.

While he cooked, Rebecca sat on the deck, staring out at the ocean. There seemed to be something on her mind but he didn't want to ask if she wasn't ready to share. Despite having made amends he sensed that something between them had changed and he couldn't put his finger on what it was. He just knew he didn't want to risk there being any tension between them. He poured the orange sauce over the sliced yams, dotted the pan with pats of butter and then slid it into the oven. After checking on the rising yeast dough for the rolls he rinsed his hands, wiping them on a cloth towel, and then went to see what she was up to.

Rebecca looked up as the sliding glass door opened and then closed. She smiled sweetly as Nathaniel dropped into the lounge chair beside her.

"How's dinner coming along?" she asked. "It smells amazing!"

"You'll get all your favorites on one plate. It's going to be the best meal you've had in ages."

"You say that about everything you cook for me."

Nathaniel laughed. "Because it's true."

Rebecca changed the subject. "I sent you the digital proof of the final menu. The chef made a few changes that you need to initial off on. When you're good with it, I'll place the order."

"The uniforms came in, too. Did you see them?"

"The little blonde waitress and the one with the large afro were trying them on earlier. I'm happy with them. Slightly sexy without being slutty and the women like them. I'm still not sure how I feel about those narrow-legged pants the guys will wear but they did look good on the men."

Nathaniel nodded. He took a deep inhale of the salt-water that misted the air, settling back in his seat.

"You're not going to burn anything in there, are you?"

"You know better, Bec. I don't burn food."

"I just wanted to be sure. You're out here and the food's cooking in there. I know if it were me, something would be bound to burn."

"Relax! I've got this, Bec."

She nodded, watching as he settled himself comfortably beside her. The moment was quiet and easy. In the distance the sun was just beginning to set, turning the horizon dusty with striations of yellows and oranges interspersed with patches of blue sky and water. It was simply breathtaking. Minutes passed and then Rebecca broke the silence that had settled between them.

"Why have you and I never dated?" she asked, the one question Nathaniel wasn't at all expecting.

He shot a look in her direction. "Date? What...? I don't..."

"You're stuttering. It wasn't a hard question, Nate. Why do you think you and I never dated each other?"

"For one, you weren't attracted to me."

She narrowed her gaze, her expression incredulous. "Really?"

"Really. And two, I don't think either of us wanted to ruin a perfectly good friendship if things didn't work out. I know I didn't. I can't imagine you not being in my life and if we dated and things went left, we might not be able to recover from that. Being around each other would be awkward so we'd stop hanging out. We might not talk to each other. It would just not be cool. Don't you agree?"

Rebecca shrugged, but she didn't bother to answer. Her silence was disquieting and suddenly had him nervous.

"What's wrong, Bec? Why are you asking? Did someone say something about us?"

"I was just curious," she muttered, her gaze shifting back over the landscape.

"It's not like you were interested in me like that, right?"

"If you say so."

"Because you weren't, were you? Interested in me in that way?"

"It was just a question," Rebecca quipped, "don't make it out to be something it's not."

"Don't play like that. You make me nervous sometimes!"

Rebecca blew a soft sigh as she turned back to stare at him. She sniffed the air, her brow furrowed. "I think something's burning," she said, pointing him back to the kitchen. "And it better not be my candied yams!"

Chapter 5

The more Rebecca thought about it the more she began to think that Nathaniel was right. Everything about their friendship worked. Why should they risk ruining perfection trying to take things to another level?

Although her attraction for him was sometimes intense, it wasn't like she couldn't handle it. She'd been dealing with her feelings for years. Regular cold showers, a standing supply of vibrator batteries and the occasional one-night stand wouldn't make much difference. Maybe, she thought, her fixation was just a passing fancy that would actually pass if she made an earnest effort to stop obsessing.

Then she wondered if they were both being foolish. Was it fear that was keeping them from taking that leap of faith? Were they missing out on something magnificent because they were both cowards? Would allowing themselves to be honest about their feelings be such a bad thing? Why would waking up together, sharing every aspect of their lives and making sweet love before falling asleep each night not be the best thing that could happen to either of them?

And making love to each other had to be everything she'd ever imagined it to be. She could just feel the sensation of his touch, his body against hers, loving her, heated, passionate, delightful in every way. She's been fueling fantasies of him for years. Thoughts of his bed and hers, the shared kisses and caresses. She slowly drew her hands down the length of her body, eventually clasping her fingers in the heat between her legs. Clearly, she mused, Nathaniel didn't know what the hell he was talking about.

They were best friends! Closer than most married people he knew. Nathaniel didn't care that he suddenly found himself wanting her more than he'd wanted any woman prior. He refused to risk ruining the bond they shared. And despite whatever Rebecca might be thinking, he knew she could do better than him. He rolled to the other side of his king-sized bed.

He hadn't been honest when he'd told her that he had never considered them dating. Truth be told he'd thought about taking their relationship farther more times than he cared to count. Timing had never been their friend though. Jeffrey had gotten in the way in the beginning.

After that had gone south, he would have been her re-bound guy, used until the hurt was gone from her sys-tem. He'd been her buddy and pal instead, supplying the tissues and the shoulder when she needed one.

Other relationships had come between them after that. Other men she'd dated; a few women he'd shared time with. Nothing serious or lasting for either of them. He'd been focused on building his medical practice and she'd been dedicated to building her own business. Time flew by before either could blink an eye. Fam-ily issues—the death of her father from cancer and his brother's injury—had sometimes prevailed and it had become easy to waylay the possibilities of being more than friends.

And truth be told Nathaniel wasn't sure he even knew how to do a serious relationship. He'd never had any examples to learn from. His own father hadn't cared to be there for his mother and she'd been angry and bit-ter about that for all her life. His focus had always been fairly narrow, dedicated to his studies, his career and his business. Rebecca deserved a man who would make her his priority and he wasn't sure he could make her that kind of promise.

But he couldn't deny that he had feelings for her. Re-becca was an amazing woman and what they shared was incredibly special. She was also sexy as hell. A stunning goddess with the spirit of an angel and attitude galore, she epitomized everything any man worth his weight in gold could want.

Now Bec was questioning why they hadn't, when he

was desperately trying to justify why they shouldn't. The more he thought about her, and them, the more conflicted he felt. He was suddenly grateful that she had insisted on going back to her hotel room after they'd polished off the last of the bourbon peach pie and that churn of vanilla ice cream that he'd made for dessert. Her staying might not have been a good idea, he suddenly thought. Because if she had been in the other bedroom, there was probably nothing that would have kept him from going to her.

Nathaniel had fallen asleep on the sofa. After tossing and turning for hours he'd gotten out of bed, poured himself a shot of bourbon and had sat in the living room watching reruns of the reality television series *48 Hours*. He didn't have a clue what the time had been when he'd finally fallen asleep. When his doorbell rang, pulling him from a deep slumber, it was still dark outside and an infomercial for a Chia puppy was playing on the television screen.

The bell rang a second time, someone leaning on it for his attention. As he stood, stretching himself up and outward, his cell phone was flashing, notifications of several missed calls blinking rapidly.

The doorbell rang again and then again. Moving swiftly, he peered out through the sidelights before pulling the entrance open. He was surprised to find Rebecca standing on the other side.

"Where's your key?"

"I told you I'm not using that key, Nate."

He shook his head. "What's wrong?"

She was dressed in shorts and a lightweight sweat top. Her hair was pulled back into a messy ponytail. Mesh-topped, rubber-soled water shoes adorned her feet. She pushed her way in, gushing too eagerly for comfort.

"There's nothing wrong. You didn't listen to my messages, did you?"

"I didn't even hear the phone ring."

"Not to worry. We still have time. But you'll need to hurry and get dressed."

He looked at his watch. She was way too chipper for the early morning hour. She was not a morning person so it was totally out of character for her. He knew something was definitely wrong.

"Bec, it's just six o'clock!"

"And the sun rises in twelve minutes. If I miss this sunrise I'm really going to be pissed, Nate! Get dressed!" she admonished a second time.

"Can't we just watch it from the patio."

"I want to walk the beach. It's on my bucket list of things to accomplish before I turn forty."

"You still have three years, Bec. Does it have to happen this morning? I didn't get a whole lot of sleep last night."

"Neither did I and no, it can't wait."

He shook his head, confusion wafting over his expression.

Rebecca snapped. "Are you doing this with me or not? Because if you don't want to I can…"

He held up his hand and stalled her comment. There was just enough attitude in her tone that he knew better than to argue. "Let me slip on my pants," he said. "It will only take me a minute."

And that was when Rebecca realized he was standing there in nothing but his underwear and a tank top. He trailed his fingers around the waistband of a pair of black boxer-briefs that hugged the bulge of his family jewels nicely. The sleeveless tank was snug against his broad chest and back. She stared unabashed, her eyes blinking in appreciation. When he turned, she gasped. Loudly. The curve of his backside was so high and tight that she suddenly wished she had a quarter to bounce off it.

It wasn't the first time she'd seen him in his skivvies. In fact, over the years she had seen him naked more than a handful of times. But each time was like Christmas, her birthday and the Fourth of July rolled into one happy moment!

It took no time at all for Nathaniel to splash water on his face, brush his teeth and slip into a pair of sweats and a T-shirt. There was just enough chill in the early morning air that he also reached for his vinyl windbreaker and pulled it over his head. He slipped his feet into a pair of leather boat shoes then moved back into the living space. He found Rebecca on the deck waiting for him.

Rebecca's exuberance was like a match igniting a gas fire. As they maneuvered the craggy path down to the sandy beach, they held hands and laughed at the absurdity. In the distance the first hint of morning light was just beginning its slow climb out of the darkness.

"So how long have you had this bucket list?" Nathaniel asked. He squeezed her fingers between his own as he clasped her palm tighter to his. Their arms swung easily between them.

She shrugged. "I say bucket list but it's not really that. It's just a list of things I want to experience and appreciate in my lifetime, not just necessarily because I'm thinking about my mortality but because I'm thinking about improving the quality of my life overall. I've never really stopped to appreciate a sunrise and I figured I couldn't find a better setting."

"What else is on this bucket but not a bucket list?"

She cut an eye in his direction, noting how intensely he seemed to be studying her. "It changes. Things get added. Things get taken off."

"Things like?"

"I want to set foot on all the continents. Swim with dolphins. Run a marathon. Well, maybe a half marathon. Learn how to pole dance."

Nathaniel laughed. "Pole dance? Really?"

"Why not? I could do it. In fact, I've already taken some classes."

"I'm not saying you can't. I'm just wondering why you would want to. Had you said ballroom or tap that would have made sense to me. But I don't see you working the pole, Bec."

"Because I'm a big girl?"

"Because you're too damn pretentious and exceptionally prissy! It goes against the grain of that image you like to protect."

"I am not that shallow."

He shook his head. "I wasn't saying that, either."

"That's what it sounded like."

"Because you're trying to pick a fight and I'm not going to let you."

"That's not what..." she started and then she hesitated, cutting the comment abruptly. There was just a moment of hesitation as she thought about what he'd said. She bit down against her bottom lip as contrition seeped from her stare.

Nathaniel smiled. "I can't wait to see you work the pole. In fact, I'm going to start saving my dollars now especially for when you do so you'll know how much I appreciate your talent. Hell, I may even work the pole with you. In fact, I think we should do this bucket list thing together. It'll be our thing."

"Now I know you fell down and bumped your head."

"Hell, you're going to make me do it anyway so I might as well just prepare myself."

Rebecca laughed this time. "What makes you think I'm going to *make* you do it with me?"

Nathaniel pulled the back of her hand to his mouth and pressed a damp kiss against it. He pointed with his other hand. "Because I'm standing on the most beautiful beach at six in the morning watching the sun come up," he said as his gaze settled on the landscape before them.

Rebecca turned to where he stared. The morning sun looked as if it was suddenly blooming, a flowering sphere unfolding petals of light as it illuminated the dark blanket that had been holding it captive just minutes earlier. It was breathtakingly beautiful. She smiled, a full grin filling her face. Joy suddenly shimmered in her dark eyes.

Her bright smile lifted his and they laughed heartily. With a slight tug he pulled her down to the white sand to sit as they watched. Rebecca leaned her head against his shoulder and allowed herself to settle comfortably against his large frame. Nathaniel leaned to kiss her forehead, brushing his lips lightly against her warm skin. An hour later when the sun had found its seat in a bright blue sky, greeting them with its warmth, they were still huddled in conversation.

Rebecca scrambled eggs and Rebecca didn't cook. At least not well. Her eggs were probably Nathaniel's least favorite thing that she did cook. Despite his dislike of them she was determined to perfect her recipe until hers were as good as his. Nathaniel was in the shower, readying himself for another day of work and she figured she'd prepare the morning meal for him since he almost always did it for her. It was the least she could do after waking him so early.

Bacon was frying and slices of thick bread rested on the counter to be toasted. She had wrestled with his coffee press, finally giving up when she couldn't get a decent cup. She'd made *horchata* instead. Simmering milk, rice and cinnamon was far easier and he liked her recipe for the frothy Mexican classic, especially when she spiked it with a hint of rum.

The aroma of bacon sizzling was beginning to waft through the air. She prepped two plates, setting the table for the two of them. In the distance she heard his phone ring. When he answered, greeting his favorite real estate woman warmly, annoyance pinched her in the side. She feigned disinterest as she strained to listen to his conversation.

"Elise, good morning! How are you?"

He paused as he listened. "I can probably swing that. I don't have any plans at the moment that I know about but let me check my schedule before I give you a definite answer."

Something was said and his response was inaudible, the buzzer on the oven drowning him out. Rebecca cussed, the profanity a loud whisper.

There was another lengthy pause before he spoke again. "Otherwise everything else is good with you?"

Rebecca took a swift inhale of air as she dropped the pan of bacon onto the stovetop, allowing it to drop harshly against the stainless steel.

Nathaniel laughed at something he found funny. She moved to the hallway and called his name. Loudly.

"Breakfast is ready, babe!"

There was a quick moment of silence before he answered. "Thanks, Bec. I'll be right there."

"Really, you're not interrupting," he said into his cell phone receiver. "I appreciate you calling to let me know."

More silence ensued and Rebecca could only imagine what was being said on the other end of the line. She was certain Elise the Realtor had some sad, sob story she hoped would win her favor with Nathaniel. Little did she know, Rebecca wasn't about to let that she-devil make any headway with her best guy. Maybe she and Nathaniel weren't meant to be in a romantic relationship but she fully intended to try. Nathaniel didn't have a clue what was about to hit him.

She heard him promise to call the woman soon before he disconnected the line. She moved to the refrigerator to return the carton of eggs and the gallon of milk. As she spun back to the counter, Nathaniel moved into the room.

"Something smells really good!" he exclaimed.

"Bacon. I do really good bacon," she said with a wink of her eye.

He laughed, taking the cup of hot beverage she held out for him. He inhaled the sweet aroma. "*Horchata!* You must have been reading my mind. I was dreaming about a cup! You do love me!"

"You had doubts?"

"Never, *babe*!" he said as he moved to the dining table to take a seat. There was a hint of sarcasm in his tone as he shot her a look. He chuckled warmly.

"So how is Elise?" she questioned, bringing up the woman since it didn't look like he planned to.

He tossed her a look. "Elise is good. She called to invite me to the next chamber of commerce meeting. We should both go."

Rebecca frowned. "You're the business owner in this here small town. Not me."

"You're as much a part of this restaurant as I am. Besides, it's a great opportunity for you to network for some new clients. I'm not going to be able to afford you forever. I'm already over budget and if you find one more thing wrong, I'll have to serve water for the first month."

"I promised you perfection and I plan to deliver perfection. Besides, you have deep pockets. Don't think I don't know that."

"You gold digger, you! It's been about my money this whole time."

His teasing tone moved her to laugh. Rebecca took a sip of her own drink. "Yep! I've been after your coins since the first day I met you when you didn't have any coins!"

"You realized my potential."

"I'm psychic that way."

"Speaking of," he shifted forward in his seat. "I need spices. You interested in taking a field trip with me?"

"We were talking about spices?"

Nathaniel grinned. "We were. You really need to keep up."

"Then I guess I am going on a field trip with you. Where are we going?"

"I'll let you know but I want to go this weekend maybe. No later than early next week though."

"Okay," Rebecca answered. She changed the subject. "How are my eggs?"

* * *

Rebecca heard the woman before she saw her. Elise had a distinctive laugh that was as irritating as fingernails against a chalkboard and the few times the two had seen each other she'd been tittering on about something. She had also gotten into the annoying habit of popping up at the restaurant whenever it suited her and fawning over Nathaniel like she was in heat and ready to breed.

All of the men found her entertaining, a pleasant distraction from whatever they were supposed to be doing. The short skirts and low cut blouses garnered her much attention. Her being a distraction was why the tile guy had to replace a huge section of the foyer flooring. And why Rebecca was constantly irritated by her presence.

Moving toward the commercial kitchen Rebecca found her leaning against the door of the new walk-in freezer. She stood with her legs crossed at the ankle, one arm crossed over her waist, her thumb tucked into the waist of her pencil skirt and her other hand playing with the pearls around her neck. She was laughing at Nathaniel like he was doing standup, each word she was hanging on cause for comedic relief. As she moved toward them she and Nathaniel locked gazes and she rolled her eyes skyward.

"Good afternoon," he chimed, his stare admonishing her to behave.

"Hello. Elise, how are you? No houses to sell today?"

Elise gave her a snide smile. "It's good to see you again, Rebecca. I thought you'd be back in Los Angeles by now."

Smiling back, Rebecca moved to Nathaniel's side, allowing her hip to gently brush against his. "I'm here for as long as Nathaniel needs me," she said.

"Then I'm sure you'll be able to head on home right after the opening next week."

"I wouldn't take bets on that if I were you."

Nathaniel cleared his throat. "What's up, Bec? I wasn't sure I was going to see you this afternoon."

"We need to review the numbers and I just want to double-check that we're still on target with our delivery dates. I have a long list of things I need to discuss with you. But you just finish your conversation. I need to check on the painter. They had the wrong color in the bathrooms and he was supposed to get that fixed."

"I actually need to be going," Elise said. "We're still on for this evening, right, Nathaniel?"

He nodded. "I'll see you at seven."

"Let's plan on grabbing dinner afterward. I have a business proposal I'd like to discuss with you."

He cut an eye toward Rebecca. "Were you joining us at the chamber meeting, Bec?"

Rebecca looked at Elise, eyeing her from head to toe and back. Amusement danced across her face. She gave Nathaniel a smile. "Sorry, I have to pass. I'm meeting Jeffrey Baylor later this evening."

"Jeffrey? You know Jeffrey Baylor?" Elise perked up with interest.

"We all went to school together," Nathaniel answered. "He and Bec were actually engaged at one point. But it didn't end well." He gave Rebecca a look, his jaw tightening.

"What a great guy! And that restaurant of his is amazing! He was interested in this space at one point," Elise said. "I would never have taken you for Jeffrey's type, Rebecca."

"His type?" Rebecca crossed her arms over her chest, her gaze narrowed tightly.

"He usually likes slim blondes. But I'm so glad you two were able to reconnect, Rebecca. Hopefully you can make amends for whatever it was you did to ruin your engagement. I just love happy endings!"

"You know, Elise…" Rebecca started, bristling slightly. The air in the room was suddenly stagnant. The tensions waging war between them was so thick it could have been cut with a dull knife. They were like two polite alley cats tossed into a burlap bag.

Nathaniel interrupted her comment as he stepped between them. "Elise, Rebecca and I need to get some work done so I can make that meeting tonight. Otherwise…"

Elise held up her hands. "Say no more! I'll get right out of your way. Rebecca, it's always a pleasure to see you!"

"I have that effect on people, Elise," Rebecca answered.

Elise forced a smile on her face. "Maybe you and Jeffrey can double-date with Nathaniel and me one day. Wouldn't that be fun! If things work out with you two, of course."

"Maybe, and that's assuming things work out with you and Nathaniel. Of course."

Rebecca smiled sweetly as Elise's jubilant expression turned downward into a deep frown. "Have a good day," she said and then she turned, moving toward the office.

When Nathaniel moved into his office Rebecca was still seething. They locked eyes and he could actually feel the venom spewing in the look she gave him. He instinctively went on the offense.

"I don't know why you let that woman get under your skin."

"Not his type? She hopes I can make amends? Did that twit actually think she could throw shade and walk away unscathed? She's lucky I didn't snatch that twelve-dollar weave out of her head!"

Nathaniel laughed. "I think she paid more than twelve dollars. Actually I'm not even sure it's a weave now that I think about it."

"Are you purposely trying to piss me off even more?"

"No, I'm trying to let you know that you don't have anything to worry about. I have no interest in Elise."

"But you're having dinner with her tonight."

"And you have a date with Jeffrey. Let's talk about that."

Rebecca shifted her eyes from his, looking every-where around the room but at him. "It's not a date," she quipped. "I told him I'd meet him for coffee."

"So when were you going to tell me about that?"

"You say that like I've been sneaking around with him and keeping it a secret."

"Weren't you?"

"No. He called right before I saw you and I was going to see if you would join us but you were too busy making dinner plans with Eloise!"

"Elise."

"I know what the cougar's name is!" Rebecca countered with another eye roll.

Nathaniel laughed. "You know she has nothing on you, right? You run circles around that woman."

"I don't need you trying to flatter me now, Nate. You didn't have anything to say when that cheap trick was trying her best to insult me."

"What did you want me to do? Did you want me to smack her?"

"No, I wanted you to let me smack her!"

"We can't smack people, Bec. That's not the kind of publicity we want for the restaurant. Besides," he moved to her side and draped his arm around her shoulder, "you would not look good in a prison jumpsuit. Orange is not your color!"

Chapter 6

Nathaniel remembered a time in their lives when Rebecca would have lashed out when slighted, reacting instead of responding. He would have had to pick Elise up off the floor for far less. Back then, they had both been young and dumb and Rebecca's fuse has been exceptionally short. He was actually proud of how well his girl had handled herself. But Elise insulting Rebecca had rubbed him the wrong way and he fully intended to let her know.

As he exited the Cima Collina Winery where the monthly mixer had been held he paused to take in the view. The winery and ranch were located a short ten minutes from Carmel-by-the-Sea, in Carmel Valley. There were mountains in the distance, a valley below them, and everything was abundantly green. The fragrant scent of grapes permeated the air and everything about the landscape reminded him of just how blessed he was.

Long gone were the days of poverty when he and his siblings had gone without more times than any of them cared to count. Childhood had been difficult at best, despite the earnest efforts of his single mother who sometimes had trouble holding it together. What Norris Jean Stallion had done successfully, though, was to instill drive and determination into each of her children. She'd also insured they supported and trusted each other. Loyalty was expected and given unconditionally. He and his siblings had made her proud with their many accomplishments and for just a moment, he was missing her. Wishing she could be there the day he opened his new business venture.

As he thought about the women in his life he realized there was no way he could have ever told Elise how he felt about his mother and was needing her now as much as he did. On the other hand, Rebecca knew without him having to say the words. She instinctively knew when he wanted a moment of space and when he didn't.

His thoughts were suddenly interrupted, Elise calling his name. He turned just as she came through the door and down the steps toward him.

"Nathaniel! You didn't wait for me!"

"I didn't go anywhere, Elise. I just stepped outside. You were talking to one of your friends and I didn't want to interrupt."

Elise looped her arm through his. "So, I thought we could have ourselves a romantic dinner and then maybe after, we could…"

"I can't, Elise. I'm sorry."

"What now? I thought you'd cleared your schedule tonight?"

"To be honest, Elise, I've been giving it a lot of consideration and I think that you and I can probably be friends, but I don't see our relationship going any farther than that. So, there really is no reason to waste your time, or mine."

Elise blinked her eyes rapidly as she took in his comment. "I don't understand," she finally said. "I thought…"

He got right to the point. "I was turned off by your snide comments toward Rebecca this afternoon. She didn't deserve that from you."

"She started it! You act like she's so innocent."

"I don't recall her being snarky and trying to body-shame you about your size or thinking it was okay to critique your relationships, but I do remember you being bitchy toward her. And unnecessarily so. It put her on the defensive and I didn't appreciate that."

Elise flipped a dismissive hand at him. "It was all in jest. I'm sure Rebecca didn't take any of it seriously."

"Well, I did and bottom line, I can't see myself in a relationship with someone who has mean girl tendencies."

Elise looked as if she'd bitten into something sour, her mouth twisting unnaturally. Her eyes were blinking rapidly and it looked like she was searching for a witty comeback but simply couldn't find one. She tossed her black hair over her shoulder, her arms crossed tightly over her chest.

Nathaniel smiled. "I really should be going. Enjoy your evening, Elise," he said.

The choice names Elise called him as he headed to his car gave Nathaniel reason to smile. One or two of those names Rebecca had used often; the difference between them was that she always followed it with, *but I still love you!*

Rebecca sat across the table from Jeffrey wondering if Nathaniel was relishing his time with his new pal Elise. She couldn't stop herself from imagining the worst. The two of them cuddled up together as Elise whispered in Nathaniel's ear, and him enjoying it. The visual had her highly agitated and much annoyed.

She twisted around in her seat, leaning left and then right as she crossed her legs one way and then the other. She was antsy, anxious to get as far from Jeffrey and his own wandering eye as quickly as she could.

"You did that a lot when we were together," she said.

"What's that?"

"Ignore me as you stared at other women's asses."

He chuckled. "I don't think I did that, Rebecca."

"You're still doing it," she said as she gestured toward the redhead. "And it's still annoying and highly disrespectful."

"Then I apologize because I would never want to

offend you like that. You've always meant too much to me."

"So, what did you want to talk to me about?" she asked, seeming to have regained his attention.

Jeffrey stole one last glance at a tall redhead who had stopped to ask for a selfie and an autograph. He gave Rebecca an award-worthy smile of picture-perfect veneers as she rolled her eyes in annoyance.

"So, I'm surprised you and your Stallion aren't married with ten kids by now. When you chose him over me I figured marriage was next for you both."

"I didn't..."

He held up his hand to stall her comment. "It felt like you did but that's neither here nor there. I'm divorced now. You're single. Clearly, it's never going to happen with you and your boy. So, why not try to recapture what we used to have with each other?"

"Maybe because what we had with each other really wasn't all that good?"

He chuckled.

"I missed you, Becky. I didn't realize how much until I saw you the other day."

"My name's Rebecca. Please don't call me Becky."

"You used to like when I called you Becky."

"I was also nineteen. Young and dumb and still searching for a happily-ever-after fairy tale. I'm not nineteen anymore."

"So you've given up on your happy ending?"

"Let's just say I don't believe in fairy tales anymore."

"That makes me sad, Rebecca."

"Why?"

"Because all I ever wanted was for you to be happy."

The moment was suddenly awkward and Jeffrey reached across the table for her hand, gently caressing the back of it. She was suddenly uncomfortable with the familiarity of his touch. It felt foreign, like a lost memory that didn't quite make sense. Rebecca slowly slid her hand away from his.

She stood abruptly. "I'm sorry. This wasn't a good idea."

"What's wrong? I don't understand."

"I just shouldn't be here, but thank you for the coffee."

"Don't leave, Rebecca. We need to talk."

Rebecca shook her head. "No, we really don't," she said and then she raced for the door, not even bothering to toss one last look over her shoulder.

Beginning to sound like a broken record Rebecca practiced what she planned to say to Nathaniel when she next saw him. She repeated her thoughts over and over again in her head. *I don't want to be your friend. I don't want to just be your friend. I want to be more than your friend. I think we should be together. I love you…*

Her phone chimed, announcing another incoming message. She didn't bother to look, knowing it was only Jeffrey and Jeffrey could be exceptionally persistent.

She blew a soft sigh. She didn't know what she'd been thinking when she'd agreed to meet Jeffrey. A part of her had hoped to maybe make Nathaniel jealous. And a part of her had wanted to make sure she was truly over the man who'd once been at the top of the list to be her husband. She had often wondered what would have become of them together had she said yes and gone with him to France when he'd asked. More important, what would have come of her and Nathaniel if she'd given up on the fantasy she sometimes allowed herself about the two of them. Because everything would have changed if she had put Jeffrey first, their friendship redefined. Becoming something she couldn't begin to fathom. Would she and Nathaniel still have even been friends?

What the last few days had shown her, though, was that Jeffrey had definitely not been the one. Despite his best efforts he was smoke and mirrors with little substance. He fell back on smooth lines and innuendo when something more substantive was needed. He was bubblegum that lost its flavor after only a few chews. Had she gone to Europe they would probably be divorced. And even in that scenario, what she trusted most was that Nathaniel would have been there to support her through it all.

Suddenly it was all too complicated and it really didn't need to be. She was past ready to get off the roller coaster she and Nathaniel seemed to be riding. She was ready for her future and hopeful that he would want that with her. But she wasn't going to know if she never opened up and told him how she felt.

She had not heard from Nathaniel and she couldn't help but wonder if he and that woman were still together. Their meeting should have been long over but she had no doubts Elise would try to extend her time with the man. Rebecca knew that under the same circumstances she surely would have.

Looking around, she saw the hotel parking lot had begun to fill. It was later than she realized. She restarted the ignition and pulled her car back onto the main thoroughfare. She fully intended to disturb any plans Elise might have for Nathaniel tonight.

Nathaniel had only been home for a few short minutes when his doorbell rang. He had thought about calling Rebecca to see how her coffee date had gone with Jeffrey and then he'd changed his mind. She needed to get whatever it was about him out of her system. At least that was what his sisters had advised.

Calling Naomi and Natalie for advice had come with a side order of crow. He hated admitting they were right and they'd been telling him for years that what he and Rebecca shared was more than simple friendship. Both his sisters, and his brothers, had labeled his relationship when he wasn't interested in labels. Romance hadn't been high on his priority list and he'd had absolutely no desire to be distracted by that thing they called love. Now, Rebecca was a bigger distraction than he could have ever imagined.

He knew he would hear from her eventually. Despite his desire to call he didn't want it to seem like he was too anxious, or worried, about her and Jeffrey being together, even if a small part of him was.

Back in the day Jeffrey had been that dude who could

talk an ice queen into his heated drawers. He was too smooth and they'd all lost count of the many women that had fallen for his charms. When Rebecca had fallen and fallen hard, it had surprised him. And it had hurt. She had deserved better and it seemed nothing he said could convince her of that. When Jeffrey had promised her a life of excitement and glitz starting in Paris, Nathaniel had prepared himself to say goodbye. When she stayed, he had promised her, and God, that she could always depend on him. No matter what.

The ringing doorbell moved him to smile, hopeful that Rebecca had cut her evening short. He only wished she'd start using the key he'd given her. Pulling the entrance open he was surprised to find Elise standing on the other side of the door. His shock showed on his face and she called him out on it.

"No, it's not Rebecca."

"Elise! Did you follow me home?"

"I didn't like how we left things."

"You mean you screaming obscenities at me as I pulled out of the parking lot?"

"I mean I was hoping you'd give me a few minutes of your time to make amends."

"I don't think…" Nathaniel started.

"Please?" She batted her lashes, her doe eyes begging.

Nathaniel took a deep breath and stepped back, gesturing her inside as he closed the door after her. He was suddenly hit with the thought that her being there in his home was probably not a good idea.

Elise moved through the entrance into the living space, seeming quite comfortable. He followed, his own anxiety level rising abruptly.

"I'm sorry, Elise. I'm not sure what there is for us to say to each other. I don't want there to be any bad feelings between us but I can't help how I feel."

Elise spun around on her high heels to face him. "First, I want to apologize. I've behaved badly. You called me out on it and then I was in my feelings about it. You didn't deserve me ranting at you the way I did. I hope you'll accept my apology."

He nodded. "I appreciate that. I hope you will extend the same courtesy to Rebecca."

Elise gave him a smile but she didn't bother to affirm his statement. She took a step toward him instead, pressing her fingertips to his chest. "I know you think things between us couldn't work but I think you're wrong. I think you and I would be very good together. And I think you should take a chance before you count me out."

Nathaniel shook his head. "I thought I made myself perfectly clear?"

"Maybe this will help you change your mind," Elise said. She took a step back, slowly untying the belt that closed her wrap dress. The garment opened to expose a pink satin camisole and matching panty. She let the dress slide to the floor, standing with her hands clutching her narrow hips.

He suddenly stammered. "I don't… I'm not…this isn't…"

It was just then that his front door swung open, Rebecca using that key for the first time. She called his name as she moved through the foyer and then she came to an abrupt halt, stunned to see the two of them standing there.

Nathaniel stood dumbfounded, his mind suddenly mush. "Bec, hey!" he finally muttered as Elise grappled to restore her clothes. "What took you so long?"

As Rebecca stood staring at him and then Elise in most of her glory, and back to him, all she could do was laugh. And laugh she did. A gut-deep chortle that soon had her doubled over with tears streaming down her face. And Nathaniel was laughing heartily with her.

"I still don't know what was so funny," Rebecca said. She pulled her knees to her chest as she leaned back against the pillows of the sofa cushions.

Nathaniel shrugged as he filled a large bowl with freshly popped popcorn that he drizzled with white truffle oil and tossed with a dash of parsley and freshly grated parmesan cheese. After filling two glasses with white wine he carried the lot on a wooden tray into the family room and settled himself on the sofa beside her.

Rebecca took a sip of the sparkling Chenin Blanc. After nibbling on two handfuls of the popcorn she resumed their conversation. "We owe your girlfriend an apology. She was pretty upset when she left here."

Nathaniel heaved a deep sigh. "Elise is some sort of special. Which is why she's not my girlfriend."

"I shouldn't have laughed, though, but the expression on your face was priceless. I wish I'd gotten a picture."

"I'm glad you didn't. So, how was your date?"

Rebecca smiled. "I left before they poured my coffee."

"That wasn't cool and you two had so much to catch up on." The smug expression on Nathaniel's face moved her to laugh again.

"No, we really didn't," she said. "It wasn't at all what I thought I wanted it to be. There were no amazing revelations. It took all of two minutes for me to realize that I already knew everything I needed to know."

Nathaniel shoved his hand into the bowl of popcorn and grabbed a fistful. He shoved the seasoned kernels into his mouth. "Well I'm glad you figured out he was a jerk. I've been telling you that for years." He yawned, stretching his body outward. "This has been a very long day."

"Nate, we really need to talk," Rebecca said softly. She shifted her body against the pillows.

"Yeah, sure. Whatever you want, Bec!"

"Well, I've been really thinking about the two of us lately. You know you're my best friend."

"And you're mine," Nathaniel interjected. "You know me better than I know myself sometimes. You're the best friend I've ever had."

Rebecca smiled. "Which is why I don't understand why it's so hard for me to say what I want to say." She rambled, trying to stall her nerves. Her speech from earlier was a lost memory as she struggled to remember the words she had practiced over and over. So, she poured her heart out, one lengthy run-on sentence gushing through the air. She finally closed her eyes and took a deep breath. "Nate, what I'm trying to say is…"

Before she could complete her comment, Nathaniel snored loudly. Just that quickly he had fallen sound asleep and was resting comfortably at the other end of the sofa. Rebecca shook her head from side to side. *It never failed*, she thought, *Between them it didn't seem like they would ever get it together!*

They woke abruptly, startled out of their sleep when the alarm on Nathaniel's watch chimed loudly. They were tangled together on the sofa, legs intertwined one over the other.

Nathaniel ran a warm palm along her calf. "Good morning, Bec."

"What's so good about it?" Rebecca responded. She yawned, stretched and rolled into the pillows.

"We're going shopping," he answered.

"Is that today?"

"It is. We need to get up and get dressed. Our flight leaves in an hour."

Rebecca sat up, confusion washing over her face. "Flight? I thought we were just going to go buy spices and groceries for the restaurant?"

"We are."

"So, why do we have to take a flight?"

"Because where we have to go shopping requires an airplane for us to get there, Bec."

"Excuse me? An airplane?"

"Catch up, Bec! You're usually faster than this."

"Forgive me. I haven't had my first cup of coffee yet."

Nathaniel moved onto his feet, untangling his legs from hers. "Seriously, we need to get moving. We have to stop by the hotel so we can check you out and get your things."

"Who said I'm checking out of the hotel?"

"I'm saying. Since you're finally using your key there is no reason for you not to stay here. Besides, I may need your protection in case Elise decides to show up naked again."

Rebecca laughed warmly. "I don't think you have anything to worry about there."

Nathaniel laughed along with her. "I need to grab a shower."

"So do I. I'll head over to the hotel and get dressed. Pick me up there."

"You need to pack a bag, too," he said with a nod. "Enough for a day or two."

"I can't with you," Rebecca said, her head waving from side to side. "How does going to the grocery store suddenly turn into a two-day trip out of town?"

He shrugged, his broad shoulders pushed toward the ceiling. An exceptionally wide grin spread from ear to ear across his handsome face. "By the way, did we ever finish that conversation you wanted to have last night? Because I don't remember much of what happened after the popcorn and wine."

Rebecca met the look he was giving her with her own. She thought back to the conversation she had apparently had with herself. She smiled, her head bobbing ever so slightly. "We're good," she said softly.

"Are you certain? It sounded like it was important to you."

Rebecca paused for the briefest moment and then she said, "I'm sure," her own grin as wide.

Chapter 7

The long-range, Gulfstream G650 jet waiting on the tarmac exceeded Nathaniel's wildest dreams. He suddenly thought about Rebecca's apples and oranges statement. He clearly owed his sister-in-law, Catherine Moore-Stallion, far more than dinner in his new restaurant. Catherine or Cat, as the family called her, owned a multimillion-dollar aircraft leasing company and had been very generous with her resources. He was going to have to cater her and his brother Noah's baby shower, their kid's sweet sixteen and his niece or nephew's wedding, to repay their generosity.

Both he and Rebecca boarded the plane with wide eyes and gaping mouths. The luxury aircraft had an eight-seat configuration with leather recliners, a full-sized galley and lavatory. It afforded them comfort and amenities that they hadn't even begun to imagine.

The flight attendant greeted then warmly. "Dr. Stallion, Ms. Marks, welcome aboard!" the tall, lanky man said. He relieved them of their luggage and pointed them to seats of their choosing. "My name is Brian and I'll be traveling with you this morning. Can I interest either of you in a beverage before we take off?"

"I would love a glass of mimosa, if that's possible," Rebecca said. "A pineapple mimosa, actually!"

"A pineapple mimosa? Really?" Nathaniel said with a slight laugh. "It's not even nine o'clock yet!"

"You have me flying millionaire-class. That means millionaire goodies!" Rebecca quipped. "Unless you don't have mimosas?" She looked to Brian with a raised brow.

Brian smiled. "That won't be a problem, ma'am. And for you, sir?"

"Well, in that case, I think I'll have a pineapple mimosa, too!"

"Coming right up. Please, make yourselves comfortable and I'll be right back."

"But no mimosas for the pilots!" Rebecca chimed after him. "Not until we land!"

The other man laughed as he gestured with a thumbs-up.

Rebecca dropped down into one of the plush seats. "So, you still haven't told me where we're going."

Nathaniel grinned. "Morocco!"

Her eyes widened as she turned to stare at the man. "Morocco?"

He nodded. "We'll be there in approximately twenty-one hours. We have a quick stop in Paris first to refuel and then on to Marrakesh. We'll shop one, maybe two days and then we'll come right back."

Rebecca laughed, clapping her hands excitedly. "This is insane!"

"It probably is," her friend said as he dropped into the seat beside her. "But what's a little adventure between friends?"

Brian moved back to their sides, two tall flutes of champagne and pineapple juice in hand. "The pilot says we'll be taking off in about twenty minutes. He'll be turning on the seat belt sign soon and I'll come back for your glasses when he does. I'll gladly bring you another once we reach our cruising altitude."

"Thank you," Nathaniel said.

"How fast does this baby go?" Rebecca asked, her energy level suddenly sky-high.

"Near the speed of sound, I do believe."

She smiled. "Wow! That's fast!" she said cheerily.

Nathaniel laughed. He was equally excited and feeling very confident about his decision. He suddenly shifted forward in his seat, concern washing over his expression. Rebecca's face had dropped into a downward frown, something amiss in her eyes. She jumped from her seat, the gesture abrupt.

"Bec, what's wrong?" he asked.

"I can't go to Morocco! I can't leave the country! I

have to get off this plane!" She was moving from side to side, her hands moving as frantically as her mouth.

"Woman, what the hell are you talking about?"

"I don't have my passport! I can't travel without my passport. I don't know what you were thinking!"

He laughed again as he stood up and moved to her side, grabbing her by the shoulders. "I was thinking that if you can talk to my sisters when it suits you, that I could talk to your sister when necessary. I had her express-mail me your passport earlier this week. You will have no problems getting into and out of the country."

"Really?"

"Bec, you don't think I'd do this without you, do you?"

"I don't know what to think, Nathaniel Stallion. When it comes to you and me...well..."

He took a step closer to her, shifting his weight and warmth nearer to her. He clasped her hands between his own, entwining their fingers together. "It's like you were saying last night, the bond between us is practically sacred. You are as much a joy and a blessing in my life, as I am in yours. We're good together and it has scared the hell out of us both. But it's time we stopped being scared. We're missing out on the best thing that could happen to either of us. And like you said, I don't want to miss out on anything more."

A slow, upward bend of Rebecca's mouth made her entire face glow. She nodded slowly. "So you did hear what I said last night."

"I heard every word, Bec."

She bit down against her bottom lip. "So what now?"

A low gust of air blew past his full lips. Nathaniel lifted her hands and kissed the backs of her fingers. His touch was gentle, his lips like silk against her skin as he kneaded the flesh softly. "Well," he said softly, his voice a low whisper. "Right now, I'm going to kiss you and I don't plan on giving you a little friendly peck on the lips. I plan to kiss you like I mean it, and I expect..."

Rebecca pulled her hands from his and laced them around his neck. She pushed her body against his, allowing her soft curves to fold sweetly against his hard lines. "So just kiss me already!" she said and then he did, claiming her mouth with his.

Soon, kissing Rebecca became Nathaniel's all-time favorite thing to do. She tasted like fresh mint and pineapple mingled with sugared candy as he teased the line of her teeth with his tongue. Her lips were full and plush, the sweetest cushions against his own. She opened her mouth to let him in and their tongues danced together slow and easy. Every kiss was searching, a new discovery as they explored what both had only dreamt of prior. He found it intoxicating. In that moment he knew he would never again pass up any opportunity to kiss his beautiful Bec. And she was his, heart and soul. As he kissed her he realized she always had been.

The flight to Paris Charles de Gaulle Airport took just over ten hours. When they landed for refueling they were both exhausted, having talked nonstop for most of the trip. Nathaniel had been amused as Rebecca called herself negotiating the parameters of a relationship they had already defined many years earlier.

"You know I'm funny about my personal space. And sometimes I just need me time. I don't want you to take that personally."

Nathaniel laughed. "It's never been a problem before, Bec. I'm sure it'll be fine now."

"I'm obsessing, aren't I?"

"You do that sometimes."

"Aren't you nervous at all? Because I'm scared to death that we're going to mess things up. We have such a wonderful friendship and if this goes south we might not be able to recover from it."

"No," he said leaning to kiss her again. "I'm in love with my best friend. I have nothing to be nervous about and neither do you. So stop!"

Tears misted Rebecca's eyes. Nathaniel loved her. He was in love with her. Life couldn't get any better than that, she thought.

The pilot landed the plane and then pulled the aircraft up to the hangar. Once the seat belt sign was disengaged Brian moved to update them.

"You'll have some time," he said. "We're changing pilots and refueling so we'll be here for an hour or so. Ms. Moore has arranged dinner for you. We can set it up here inside the plane or if you prefer, we can set the table up inside the hangar. It's your choice."

Nathaniel gave her a look. "It's your choice, Bec. Whatever you want is fine with me."

Rebecca's smile was bright. "Why don't we get off

and take our break in the hangar. I really do need to stretch my legs."

"It sounds like we'll be dining in the hangar," Nathaniel said as he gave Brian a nod.

"Yes, sir. It will only be a few minutes more and then you'll be able to disembark."

"Thank you," Nathaniel said. "We appreciate your efforts, Brian."

"Does Cat always arrange dinner in Paris for her clients?" Rebecca questioned.

"I guess it depends on the clients," Nathaniel said with a chuckle.

"Did you know about this?"

"No. It's news to me. But I'm sure it's no big deal, probably just sandwiches and more of those chocolate chip cookies you've been eating since you got on the plane."

"You're the one who's been obsessing over the chocolate chip cookies," Rebecca quipped. "How many have you had? I know I've only had three."

Nathaniel laughed. "Three more than I've had!"

"Don't play me! You are not going to make me feel guilty about eating cookies. I'm on vacation and I plan to eat."

"This is not vacation. We're supposed to be working, remember?"

"You're supposed to be working. I'm just tagging along for the fun. I don't even know what we're here to buy."

"Spices. Morocco is renowned for its spices. Cayenne, cinnamon, turmeric, ginger and saffron. Definitely the saffron. Those are just a few of the spices that I plan to take back with me."

Rebecca smiled. "So you did decide to do the tagine chicken?"

"I did. I'm going to make it a special for opening day. If it's well received, we may add it to the menu permanently. I'm not sure yet."

"I really love your tagine chicken!" Rebecca exclaimed as she thought about the exotic warm stew he often made for her when she needed comfort food. It was made with chicken and yams, carrots, garbanzo beans and tomatoes seasoned with garlic and coriander.

"I know you do. That's why I think we'll probably be adding it permanently to the menu at some point. Maybe call it Bec's Tagine."

"No, I think you should just let it be a special. I don't want everyone to be able to just get it every day."

"But it's so easy to make."

"But it's special. You've always made it for me when I needed a hug." The look she gave him was suddenly pulling at his heartstrings. Nathaniel understood without her needing to say the words. Over the years there were things that had become special to the two of them. Simple gestures that solidified their feelings for each other without them having to say the words. It worked when neither of them had realized why.

The moment was interrupted as Brian made his way back to their side. "Everything's ready when you are," he said softly. "You can follow me now if you like."

With a nod of his head Nathaniel reached for Rebecca's hand, clasping it gently beneath his own. He kissed the back of her fingers gently. Together, they followed their new favorite flight attendant off the airplane.

They were met at the airplane's door by a woman from immigration. After confirming their identities and reviewing their passports she welcomed them to Paris.

"I didn't know you spoke French," Rebecca said as they descended the airplane stairs and followed Brian into the private flight hangar.

"It's high school French and I really don't speak it well. I haven't had a whole lot of opportunity to practice."

"It was kind of sexy," Rebecca said, her voice dropping to a seductive tone. "Actually, it was very sexy."

Nathaniel grinned. "I'm good like that," he said as he kissed her again.

They both came to an abrupt stop, staring at the inside of the hangar. Everything was bright and shiny, the massive beams enhanced by a bright white concrete floor and large expanses of glass. A number of Fly-High Dot Com aircraft were parked pristinely in the steel-framed structure, adding to the impressive view.

Catching sight of the spread that had been laid out for them, they were both taken by surprise. Dinner was surely more than sandwiches and cookies. Someone had arranged a gourmet feast at a table set for two. Fine china and expensive crystal adorned a lace tablecloth. There was a centerpiece of fresh flowers, pillar candles and a bottle of wine waiting to be uncorked. The decadent aroma of hot food scented the air and suddenly they were both hungry.

"This is beautiful!" Rebecca gushed, wide eyes trying to take it all in.

"It's definitely something," Nathaniel responded. He turned, a slight hand waving for Brian's attention. "Did you say my sister-in-law arranged this?"

"I believe there's a card somewhere for you, Mr. Stallion," Brian said as he gestured toward the table. He moved to pull out Rebecca's seat.

Rebecca saw the small envelope perched in the leaves of the centerpiece. She pulled it from its nesting spot and waved it in the air. "Can I open it?"

Taking the seat across from her Nathaniel nodded. "Please."

The white envelope had both their names printed neatly in gold ink. Rebecca slid her thumb under the seal and then pulled out the notecard inside. She read it quickly and smiled, tears pressing against her dark lashes.

"Who's it from?" Nathaniel asked, not sure if he should be concerned or not. He extended his hand and reached for the card.

"We're excited for your future together! May this be the beginning of great things to come," he read aloud. It was signed by all his siblings.

"I really do like your family," Rebecca said as she met his stare.

He nodded. "Yeah. I think I might keep them."

* * *

Nathaniel was sleeping soundly in the leather recliner beside her. He snored loudly, his head tossed back as he rested with one arm above his head and the other draped over his chest. Rebecca shifted in her own seat, turning so that she could face him. She'd been watching him for the last hour as they flew the final leg of their trip into Morocco.

Rebecca couldn't begin to believe how happy she was. It was as if she'd been flooded with an abundance of joy. She kept expecting that she would wake and discover it was all a dream. She couldn't help but think that maybe it was all too good to be true. She heaved a deep sigh as she continued to consider it all.

Had they never left the airport in Paris she would've still been happy. That experience itself was a dream come true. Unexpected, exciting and immensely fulfilling.

His sisters had arranged a gourmet meal catered by the renowned Arpege restaurant. They dined on multicolored vegetable ravioli, Thai crab curry, couscous with vegetables and shellfish, and sea scallops in a velvety crème sauce. A hazelnut and praline torte had completed the meal and champagne flowed like water. The servings were not only pretty, looking like they'd been taken from the pages of a food magazine, but also an orgasmic experience against her tongue. Even Nathaniel, who could sometimes be a food snob, had been impressed.

They had bantered back and forth like they always

did, yet their comfort levels seemed heightened even more. It was amazing how quickly things between them had changed and had also stayed the same. He was still the love of her life but now he knew it. She had his heart and if she were honest with herself, she had always had it.

They'd departed soon after the meal ended. Hand in hand they had reboarded the plane and had settled down comfortably for the remainder of the flight. With a few more hours of flight time ahead of them, he'd fallen asleep quickly, the plush seats rocking him into a deep slumber. Rebecca had dozed slightly, waking when they'd hit a slight patch of turbulence. Unable to fall back to sleep she'd been watching him ever since, marveling at how crazy happy she was feeling. And wondering how soon it would be before everything blew up.

Morocco was extraordinary, the exotic destination nothing like Rebecca had imagined. It was late night when they finally landed. Nathaniel had reserved two adjoining rooms at the La Maison Arabe in Marrakesh. Rebecca had stayed in beautiful hotels before but this one exceeded her wildest fantasies. Expensive furniture and lush tapestries decorated his room and hers. There were two large swimming pools, a patio adorned with olive trees and rose bushes and magnificent views from their windows.

After they checked into the hotel, a bellman had guided them to their respective rooms. Once each had received their luggage, the exterior doors were closed and locked, Nathaniel had opened the door that connected the two rooms together.

"And you wanted separate rooms because…?" Rebecca said eyeing him curiously as she stepped into his space.

"Because I wanted to make sure you are comfortable. I didn't want to make any assumptions about our living arrangements. Besides, I'd reserved the hotel before you expressed your undying love for me." He grinned sheepishly.

Rebecca laughed. She didn't want to admit it but she was glad he hadn't canceled the second room. They still had things to talk about before taking their relationship to the next level. Suddenly the prospect of actually making love to him had her on edge. But she promised herself she wasn't going to agonize over it. It wasn't like the two of them didn't fall asleep together on his living room sofa every night anyway.

After a long hot shower Rebecca slipped into flannel pajamas. They were her favorite pair and the least sexy nighttime garments she owned. She toyed with the lace camisole and G-string that she'd brought with her but decided at the last minute that it wasn't the right time. When Nathaniel called her name to check on her, she stole one last glance in the full-length mirror and joined him in his room. He was seated in the center of the bed, his legs extended and crossed at the ankles. He sat with a notebook in his lap and an ink pen in his hand.

"What are you up to?" she questioned.

Nathaniel tapped an empty spot on the bed beside

him. "Just double-checking my shopping list. I need to make sure we leave here with everything we need and at least a good three- to six-month supply. And we're not going to be here long enough to do any serious price comparisons, so I need to practice my haggling skills."

Rebecca jumped onto the bed beside him. She was suddenly bubbling with exuberance. "Haggling! You know that's right up my alley, right! I am the queen of making a deal."

"I do. Why do you think I brought you along?"

"You brought me along because I'm such wonderful company."

"That, too."

Rebecca pulled his notes from his hands and read through his list. "Is this everything?"

"I think so. I was just going over it again to make sure."

"I am so excited for you," Rebecca said softly. "Your dreams are coming true. You'll soon be running my favorite restaurant and sharing the experience with your favorite girl. I am very proud of you. I hope you know that."

"I do," Nathaniel answered. He leaned to kiss her lips, cupping his palm against her cheek. "And I hope you know that I could not have done any of this without you. From the start you have been my biggest supporter. You had faith in me when I didn't have faith in myself. I love you for that. I love that you just let me be me even when I might have been getting it wrong. You mean the world to me, Bec. Please, don't ever doubt that."

The kiss he wrapped her in was sweet and easy, the gentlest caress of skin against skin. His mouth danced against hers, his lips like full, plush pillows. He slid his arm around her waist, his large hand pressing against the soft curves of her back. He eased her gently down against the bedding, his mouth urgent and possessive. For the next few minutes they made out like teenagers. Nathaniel pulled himself from her when the muscles below his waist tightened so intensely that he thought he would burst. He palmed his male member as he shifted his body from hers.

Rebecca lifted herself up on her elbows. Her breathing was static and she panted lightly. She giggled softly.

"What's so funny, Bec?" Nathaniel asked.

She gestured with her head toward his crotch. "I wore my granny panties and flannel jammies so that you'd be turned off."

Nathaniel laughed heartily. "Woman, you are sexy in everything you wear. Although the granny pants might be a little iffy, I think the flannel is hot. There is absolutely nothing about you that turns me off."

Rebecca laughed with him. After a few minutes she said, "I know you've had a hard-on for me for a while now, but I don't want you to hurt yourself trying to get that first taste. You don't know if you can handle all this yet," she said teasingly.

Nathaniel shook his head, amusement seeping out of his eyes. "Seriously now, what's really bothering you?"

She inhaled swiftly and held the air deep in her lungs

before responding. "Are you ready for us to go there? To take things to that next step so quickly?"

He pondered her question for a quick minute. The look he gave her was so intense that her breath caught in her chest and she gasped loudly. They both took a deep breath at the same time.

Finally, he spoke. "I will be ready when you are, Bec. I have thought about making love to you for longer than you may know. I think about our being together and me being inside of you all the time. But we can take this as slow as you need or as fast as you want."

Rebecca smiled. "Let's get a good night's rest so that we are both at our best tomorrow. Then tomorrow night I'll wear satin."

Nathaniel grinned. "I like satin, too."

The next day Rebecca discovered that Marrakesh was one of the busiest cities in Africa. It was a major economic center and tourist destination. Real estate and hotel development in Marrakesh was substantial and the thriving metropolis was a popular vacation spot with French celebrities. She was duly impressed when Nathaniel recognized the actor Omar Sy having dinner with friends in one of the downtown restaurants.

Marrakesh also had the largest traditional open-air market place or souk in Morocco, selling merchandise from traditional Berber carpets to modern consumer electronics. Finding the spice stalls took little effort at all. The brilliantly colored bins of food stuffs lined the aisles of the souk. Nathaniel moved swiftly to find a vendor who had been highly recommended to him. The man sat in a nondescript location toward the back end of an alleyway. He was short in stature, his skin bronzed and weathered from the sun. He wore a white linen caftan with matching slacks and a traditional Berber turban. When Nathaniel introduced himself, mentioning their mutual friend, the old man hugged him warmly, and kissed him on each cheek. He nodded politely in Rebecca's direction.

Rebecca stood aside as Nathaniel examined the spices he wanted to buy. He waved his hand in front of his nose as he inhaled the aromas, checking for product that might be stale and musty. Occasionally he took a taste to make sure the product was authentic. Minutes later he was negotiating the price of cayenne, cinnamon, cumin, sea salt, paprika, ginger and saffron. With each item the shopkeeper explained the best dishes to use which seasoning and even gave them some insight into the medicinal purposes some of the spices held.

Rebecca found herself on sensory overload with all the bright colors, weird smells and strange sounds. It felt as if they had inadvertently stepped back into another time and place. The marketplace was chaotic and overrun with tourists and it felt very much alive. Although she could have done without the skinned goat carcasses and camel heads, the occasional pile of donkey droppings and the stench of urine, she knew she wouldn't hesitate to come back again.

She and Nathaniel both enjoyed the art of bargaining the price down, sometimes as low as a third of the initial asking price. When they were done, the shopkeeper celebrated their success with an offering of mint Moroccan tea. An employee of the hotel came to take their purchases and arranged for everything to be brought back to their hotel room. The two then enjoyed a slow stroll through the souk to see all the other items being sold. By the time they made their way back to the hotel, Rebecca had purchased two Berber rugs, a half-dozen housecoats called djellabas, silver bangles and an oversized, hand-painted, ceramic tagine pot.

As they returned to their room, she asked about his purchases. "So, can you please explain to me why you paid almost four thousand dollars for that saffron? And it was just over a pound, right?"

Nathaniel nodded. "It was actually a pound and a half. I got a great deal on it. Saffron is expensive because it's difficult to cultivate. It has to be picked by hand and takes almost two hundred flowers to get one gram. He said he gets his from a town called Taliouine where it's grown."

"So what did you get the saffron for?"

"I'm doing a beautiful French bouillabaisse with sea bass, lobster and salmon. And occasionally I might do saffron potatoes."

"Are you happy with your purchases?" Rebecca asked.

Nathaniel grinned. "Are you?"

She laughed as she gestured with one of her many bags. "I could get very used to this!" she said gleefully.

Chapter 8

Nathaniel hadn't known what to expect when Rebecca called up to his room and advised that dinner was ready. After their shopping spree they had debated the where and the when for their dinner plans but were unable to come to a mutual decision. Agreeing to table the discussion until they'd showered and napped, he wasn't expecting her to have made any plans. He'd been surprised to find her gone when he woke and when she hadn't answered her cell phone he had started to become concerned.

Just when he was about ready to send out a search party the hotel room phone rang. The shrill chime, unexpected, had startled him momentarily. When he answered, Rebecca's exuberant tone greeted him from the other end.

"Where are you?" he questioned.

"Waiting for you. Are you up and dressed? If you're not, you need to throw on something comfortable and casual."

"Yes, I am dressed, but I still don't know where you are. Or where I'm supposed to be."

"I'm in the lobby," she said. "How long do you think it'll take you to come downstairs?"

"That all depends."

"On what?"

"On whether or not this little escapade is going to get me in trouble. Don't forget where we are, Bec. I do not want to be stuck in a Moroccan jail because one of your bucket list adventures goes awry."

Rebecca laughed. "How did you know that was what I had planned?"

"I know you, Rebecca Louise Marks. Better than you know yourself sometimes."

"You used my full name! You've gone serious on me."

"I'm being cautious and you need to be."

"I am being cautious. That's why we're spending the evening out and not in that room where there's a bed!"

Nathaniel laughed, amused by her candor. "What are you afraid of, Bec? Do you think I'll discover that you aren't as good in bed as you've been proclaiming for the last umpteen years?"

"I'm very good, Nate. Don't get it twisted. Just because I'm a little nervous doesn't mean I won't be the best you've ever had!"

"The proof is in the pudding. Show me, don't tell me!"

"Just come down. I'll be in the lobby waiting for you."

Nathaniel laughed again, hearing a hint of irritation in her tone. "I'll be there with bells on!"

Nathaniel didn't have a clue what to expect when he stepped off the elevator into the hotel lobby. Rebecca stood in conversation with the desk clerk, a young Muslim woman wearing an abaya and hijab. As he approached, the woman greeted him politely and lowered her eyes in deference. The cultural norm was contrasted starkly by the skyward eye roll Rebecca gave him in greeting as she leaned against the counter wearing black leggings tucked into knee-high leather boots and a lightweight sweater set.

Rebecca moved against him, adjusting the collar of his white oxford shirt. He'd paired it with denim jeans and casual brown leather slip-on shoes. He carried a tweed jacket over his arm. He was freshly shaved and smelled like her favorite Dolce & Gabbana cologne. She met his gaze, smirking slightly. Her coquettish stare was teasing and Nathaniel couldn't stop himself from chuckling under his breath.

"Good evening," he said softly as he pressed a quick kiss to her lips.

"I missed you," Rebecca said, her own voice a low whisper.

Nathaniel grinned. "So what are we doing tonight, Bec?"

Her face lit up with joy. "It's a surprise!"

With a slight wave of her hand Rebecca wished the woman she was talking to a good night, entwined her hand with his and pulled him out to a waiting car. The driver, a young man named Ahmed, greeted them both warmly as he opened the door and extended his hand to help Rebecca inside.

As Ahmed pulled the car onto the main road Nathaniel leaned forward in his seat. "So, Ahmed, what is the night life like here in Marrakesh?"

"You want party later?" the young man asked, throwing Nathaniel a look over his shoulder. His accent was thick, a broken syntax of English and Arabic scrambled together.

"Maybe," Nathaniel responded. "Are there good places here to party?"

"I like Paradise. It at Hotel Pullman Mansour Edhabi. You dance all night!" he exclaimed, his youthful exuberance gleaming across his face.

Rebecca smiled. "I could dance all night!"

Ahmed gave her a bright smile back, eyeing her through his rearview mirror. "You sing? We do karaoke at Cantobar. You do dance there, too!"

"I don't know about singing," Nathaniel said as he and Rebecca exchanged a look.

"I sing good!" Ahmed responded, and then he broke

out into a rendition of a popular song by a Moroccan pop artist named RedOne. He had a nice voice and Rebecca and Nathaniel were both entertained.

Ahmed's song came to a close just as he reached their location. His audience clapped their enthusiasm and the young man's wide smile showed his appreciation. He exited the driver's seat and hurried around to open the car door for them.

Stepping out, Nathaniel was greeted with a clear view of the desert and a massive green and orange hot air balloon that colored the dusty landscape. His gaze snapped in her direction, shock registering over his face. He suddenly tossed his head back and laughed heartily. "You're not serious, are you?" he asked after he regained his composure.

"I'm very serious, Nate" she said as they were directed closer to where the baskets sat beneath balloons being filled with hot air. There were four of them and each rose like a phoenix out of the dust, beautiful and magnificent to behold from the distance.

Nathaniel shook his head. "We really need to review this bucket list of yours a little more closely, Bec," he said.

Ahmed waved for them to follow after him. He guided them down a short path to meet their pilot who was waving at them excitedly.

"You do not want to miss the sunset!" the man said, his gregarious personality as bubbly as Ahmed's.

"I'm actually fine with watching the sunset from right here," Nathaniel said.

Giggling, Rebecca waved a dismissive hand in his direction. "Do not tell me you're afraid of heights, Nathaniel Stallion! I know better."

"You don't know everything," he muttered. "I did leave some things for you to discover."

She grinned, leaning toward him to whisper. "I'll discover those things a little later tonight," she purred.

He wrapped his arms around her shoulders and pulled her to him. Kissing the top of her head Nathaniel couldn't help but smile.

Minutes later they were enjoying a bird's-eye view of the snow-capped Atlas Mountains and the sprawling backdrop of the desert. They drifted slowly through the early evening sky, the remnants of the day's sun casting a glow of gold, orange and pink through the air. The pilot poured them glasses of champagne as he pointed out the sights below. The moment was amazing and despite his initial reservations, Nathaniel was having a wonderful time. The beauty of their surroundings took their breaths away.

They landed safely back on the ground an hour later. Just when Nathaniel thought the experience couldn't get any crazier, Ahmed was there to point them toward two camels. He cut his eyes in Rebecca's direction.

"Bucket list!" she exclaimed, laughing at his expression.

"You're killing me, Bec!" he said laughing with her. "You're really killing me here!"

"Just think of the memories we'll have to tell our grandchildren," she said matter-of-factly.

The statement suddenly gave Nathaniel reason to pause. Although he had known that one day he would marry and have children and his children would have children, it was only in that moment that he knew beyond any doubt that he would share that with Rebecca and no one else. Together they would raise a family, babies that looked like him and her. And one day he would tell their grandchildren what a wild spirit their granny had been. He would tell them about falling in love with her brand of crazy and how her unbridled spirit brought him so much joy.

He was suddenly overcome with emotion. Reaching for her, he pulled her into his arms and hugged her closely, fighting back tears that threatened to rain out of his eyes.

Rebecca hugged him back. There was something about the moment that captivated everyone's attention and both were suddenly blushing profusely as Ahmed, his associates and perfect strangers cheered.

Nathaniel drew the pad of his index finger along her profile. He stared into her eyes. "I love you, Bec! I really do love you!"

Rebecca grabbed his hand and pressed a damp kiss into his palm. "I love you, too," she whispered loudly. "I love you, too!"

The camel ride was brief, moving them from their desert surroundings to a private oasis owned by an engineer from Australia who had retired there before his death. His children, who visited infrequently, had transformed the home into a private resort spot with a five-star restaurant. The property was defined by the tranquil gardens that featured bamboo groves, cacti, great palms and pools floating with water lilies. It was home to more than twelve bird species found only in North Africa. The gardens were decorated with sculpture by local artisans and the house was a menagerie of African textiles, ceramics and an incredible collection of French impressionist paintings.

Rebecca was awed by the beauty of it all, fervently extolling every minute detail. One oil painting in particular, that of an elderly Tuareg couple, nomadic Berbers who inhabited the Saharan deserts of North Africa, fascinated her, something about the imagery touching her spirit.

"They just look so happy," she said as she sat staring at it.

"They do. They look like they have years of love between them," Nathaniel responded.

They dined on couscous with harvest vegetables, a carrot and orange salad, roasted eggplant with a yogurt dip, lamb braised with kumquats, and thick slices of a beautifully dense Moroccan bread. It was a wonderful culinary experience and with each bite she could see Nathaniel taking notes.

"Did I do good?" she questioned as they finished the meal off with mint tea and a chocolate cake made with dates, roasted almonds and strawberries.

"Baby, you did great! This has been an incredible day. I've enjoyed every minute of it."

Rebecca grinned. She reached under the table and squeezed his upper thigh. "Then I imagine what I have planned for the rest of your night will be your wildest dreams come true!" she teased.

He chuckled deeply. "You're trying to make me blush, Bec! And you're doing a very good job of it."

They parted ways at the doors to their respective rooms. Nathaniel paused to give her a deep tongue entwined kiss, her body pressed tightly against the wall as he pressed his warmly against her.

"Are you sure you don't want to shower together?" Nathaniel asked. He pushed the soft waves of her hair out of her face with his hand.

"We'll do that later," Rebecca said as she pressed her palm to his chest and held her fingers down to the tight lines of his abdomen. "I won't be long," she said. "It'll be a quick shower. I just want to freshen up after our day"

"I understand completely," he said. He leaned, pretending to sniff under her armpit.

Rebecca laughed as she gave him a slight punch in the arm. "It is not like that," she said.

He laughed with her as she opened her door, slipped inside and secured it behind her. In his own room, he stripped quickly out of his clothes, leaving a trail from the door to the bathroom. The water was only lukewarm but it felt good against his skin. He lathered himself with a lightly scented bodywash, scrubbing himself from head to toe. In his mind's eye he imagined Rebecca was doing much the same thing.

Minutes later he sat on the edge of the bed debating whether or not he should dress. He swiped a plush white towel across his back and down the length of his legs. He was excited, as evidenced by the protrusion of muscle that had lengthened between his legs refusing to subside. He took a deep breath and then another, holding the air in his lungs until they burned.

The knock on the door surprised him, and he was surprised that he was surprised. For a split second he couldn't decide if he should get up and answer it. Instead, he tossed a towel over his lap and called out for Rebecca to let herself in.

Pushing the door open, Rebecca thought her legs might give way. They were rubber, shaking so vehemently that it was a true testament to her fortitude that she was still standing. She was beyond nervous, her anxiety level so high she fathomed her blood pressure had to be way off the charts.

They locked gazes the moment she stepped into the room. His stare was intense and deliberate and instantly comforting. Rebecca's mouth lifted in a mesmerizing smile that had him standing at full attention. He moved onto his feet, still holding that white towel in front of him.

She was stunning. She had pulled the length of her hair up into a messy ponytail. She wore the promised satin, a lace-edged chemise in a vibrant shade of blue. It fell midthigh with spaghetti straps and a small bow between her full breasts. Her brown skin was tinged the faintest shade of red, warmed by the heat of her shower and the rising anxiety of her nerves. She wore no makeup, her fresh face glistening, desire shimmering in her eyes.

"What took you so long?" he said teasingly. "I was starting to think that you had changed your mind."

"I thought about it," she said. "I didn't want to torture you any longer."

"I appreciate that."

"Why are you still holding that towel?" Rebecca's gaze dropped to where he was hiding himself.

Nathaniel shrugged his shoulders ever so slightly. He let the towel go, dropping it to the floor. He raised his hands and clasped his fingers behind his head. He widened his stance, allowing her full view of every sinewy fiber and hardened muscle beneath his skin.

Rebecca stood staring as she bit down against her bottom lip. He was diesel, rock-hard marble beneath brown silk skin. The view was intoxicating and she suddenly didn't know what she'd been afraid of, or why she had waited so long. Her smile crept back to her face as he gestured with his index finger, beckoning her to him. She moved slowly in his direction, slipping the thin straps off her left shoulder and then her right. As she walked into his arms, they both exhaled, sliding easily into what felt like home.

Nathaniel dropped his body back against the bed, pulling her down above him. He kissed her passionately, one hand lost in the locks of her hair, the other trailing a heated path down the length of her back until he reached the round of her backside. He caressed the curve of her hip and kneaded the fullness of her ass.

He rolled her back against the mattress, easing his body above hers. His mouth continued to dance against her lips, a slow shimmy building into a lustful tango. By the time he broke the kiss, he had pushed the satin lingerie out of his way, the fabric tangled around her waist. His mouth and hands teased her hardened nipples. They were rock-candy-hard and sweet against his tongue and he lashed at them over and over again until Rebecca let out a low moan.

Everything about her excited him. Her soft skin, the fullness of flesh beneath his hands. She tasted like summertime and sunshine, the sweetness of memories that reminded him of strawberry ice cream and lemonade. He gasped when she suddenly reached between them, her warm palm stroking him boldly. Her touch triggered a reaction that was mere degrees from being apocalyptic. Their desire was too intense to linger in the moment and he reached for the condom he'd rested on the nightstand, sheathing the length of himself quickly.

Rebecca murmured his name over and over again, the melodic chant like a whispered prayer. She parted her legs and welcomed him into her most sacred space without hesitation. Her back arched and her limbs quivered with anticipation. She trailed her tongue over his lips, along the line of his profile, plunging it into his ear. Her fingers kneaded his arms and back as she pulled him closer to her. Unbridled heat rushed between them, leaving a trail of perspiration against their skin. Sweat beaded across her brow and he lapped at the salted moisture as if to quench his thirst.

He entered her swiftly, one deep stroke that forever sealed their fates. Tears rained from her eyes and his, the intensity of the moment so remarkable that neither had words. He tried to call her name but nothing came, his voice lost deep in his chest beneath the air trapped deep in his lungs. He dropped his weight against her instead, recapturing her mouth with his own. He loved her slowly, his strokes methodic and unwavering. In and out, back and forth, faster and faster, over and over and over again.

Rebecca latched her legs around his back. She met him stroke for stroke, her body responding in kind. The satin lining of her inner walls clenched him firmly, the muscles tightening and squeezing and milking the length of him. Her entire body was spellbound, riveted as if she were possessed. It was pleasure beyond her wildest imagination.

They rode the waves of orgasmic bliss together. Her body exploded first, inciting the eruption from his. She screamed like a woman possessed, her words incoherent, the mutterings as if she were speaking in tongues.

Nathaniel felt as if he'd plunged headfirst into a bottomless cavern of pure, unadulterated pleasure. Every neuron in his body was on synaptic overload, the influx of electrical current moving every muscle to quiver with heat. His body tensed, his hips flexed and he hissed between clenched teeth. "Yes! Oh, yes! Yes, Bec, yes!"

He fell against her, gasping for air, every ounce of his energy spent. Tears and sweat mingled sweetly together. Rebecca held him tightly against her, not wanting to ever let him go. Her body continued to pulse around his, the aftermath of spasms like little reductions of pleasure determined to hang on. "I love you," Rebecca whispered into his ear. "I love you, Nathaniel Stallion, and if you ever make me wait for that again I will seriously hurt you."

The flight back to the United States was peppered with laughter. Nathaniel and Rebecca were both punch-drunk from exhaustion. Neither had slept, making love again and again until the alarm sounded for them to rise and get ready for their trip. Everything was new to them and, yet, strangely familiar in the same breath. They spent hours in discovery, learning each other's idiosyncrasies and nuances. There were games of exploration as both memorized every crease and curve of the other's body. The two could only begin to imagine what the future held for them as they realized the many fantasies they shared with each other.

"I don't like the term boyfriend," Rebecca said.

"Why not?" Nathaniel asked.

"Because you're not a boy. It sounds too much like high school."

"So what do you prefer? Do you want to call me your *man* friend?"

"That's not cute, Nate."

"There's companion, partner, lover, boy toy, or you can make it very simple. Just call me *your man*!"

"I guess that works," she said with a slight shrug.

"I plan to call you my boo thang!"

Rebecca cut her eye at him as she giggled. "Boo thang? Really?"

He leaned over his seat toward hers to kiss her lips. "It's got flava'!"

"You are so stupid!"

He kissed her again. "You will be my boo thang even when we're old and married and you've lost that girlish figure."

Rebecca laughed heartily. "I doubt that I will ever lose this girlish figure!" she said rolling her hips from side to side in her seat.

"Must be jelly 'cause jam don't shake!" Nathaniel teased as he reached to pull her into his arms.

"You are so not funny!" she exclaimed as she continued to laugh at his antics.

He nuzzled his nose into the side of her face, inhaling the aroma of her perfume. She'd been wearing the same Estee Lauder scent since before college. It was the only fragrance she'd ever worn and once, when he'd brought her something different for her birthday, she'd made him return it to the store to exchange. Now, no matter who was wearing it, whenever he smelled it he thought only of her.

"You smell good," he murmured into her ear. "Like roses and citrus."

Rebecca kissed his lips, allowing her mouth to linger just briefly. "Thank you. I took a bath today!"

"I should try that. Imagine, soap and water on a daily basis!"

"You really should try it," she teased.

Nathaniel rolled back against his seat. He stretched his arms outward, twisting his body from side to side. "I need to run or get to the gym and work out. Especially after all the food we ate."

"Exercise is so overrated!"

Nathaniel laughed. "Says the woman who never exercises."

"I exercise. I'm just not for all that hard work where you have to sweat. I do yoga, occasionally some Pilates and I walk."

"Strolling through the stores in a mall doesn't count, Bec."

"It all depends on the mall."

After the requisite layover in Paris, the two dozed off and on, chatted about everything and about nothing, and simply enjoyed each other's company. Rebecca felt Nathaniel shifting back into work mode, his focus on what he needed to do once they were back in Carmel, to ensure a smooth restaurant opening.

"All the invitations have gone out for opening day," Rebecca said. She scribbled in one of the lined composition notebooks that she favored.

"What about the food services order? Will that delivery still be on time?"

Rebecca nodded. The local distributor that would be

providing the basic foodstuffs for Nathaniel's kitchen had promised an on-time delivery. Their reputation was impeccable, the long-standing family business coming highly recommended. She felt comfortable their delivery would not be a problem but to be safe she jotted a note to remind herself to follow up with them once they returned.

"We can't open without that delivery, Bec," Nathaniel reiterated.

"I said don't worry. When do you plan to go to the farmer's market for your fresh vegetables?"

"Probably Thursday, maybe even late Wednesday. I don't want to go too early though. I want everything to be as fresh as possible. But in case they don't have something I need, I want to be sure I have time to make a substitution. I haven't connected with any of the local farmers yet. Once I'm able to establish a rapport with them I hope to be able to get same day, predawn service."

"I'm sure that won't be a problem. Your sister Naomi emailed me the names of a few farmers that she knows and respects. Two of them are in Monterey and the third is in Gilroy."

Nathaniel shifted forward in his seat. He clasped his hands together, resting his elbows against his thighs. He dropped his chin atop his fingers and blew a soft sigh. "This is really going to happen, isn't it, Bec?"

She grinned, bright white teeth engaged in her full smile. "Yes, it is. Are you excited?"

He turned his head to stare at her. "Honest?"

"Do you have reason to lie?"

He smiled, the faintest bend of his mouth lifting upward. "I'm scared to death, Bec. What if I'm making the biggest mistake of my life?"

Rebecca reached for his hands and squeezed them. "Too late to worry about that now, Nate! But if the restaurant bombs you can always go back to being the phenomenal doctor that you have always been. I'll still love you no matter what you do!"

Chapter 9

The weather that welcomed them back to Carmel-by-the-Sea left much to be desired, Rebecca thought. The cool Mediterranean climate often boasted overcast skies, the sun blocked by abundant clouds that were constantly drizzling. But this was different, an unexpected storm brewing off the Pacific coast stirring up high winds and cooler than normal temperatures. The rains were torrential, coming in sporadic waves and Rebecca found herself wishing they were back in Morocco or anywhere else but there.

She was parked in the lot for the *Carmel Pine Cone*, the town's weekly newspaper. Covering local news, politics, arts and entertainment, opinions and real estate, it had a quaint small-town news feel and reached most of the city's three thousand residents. Rebecca had dropped off the layout for the full page ad she'd purchased to announce the restaurant's opening, making the submission deadline by mere minutes. Now, she had time to kill before she needed to be back at the restaurant to join Nathaniel. He had driven to Gilroy to meet with the owner of the local farm that his sister had recommended.

The rains suddenly eased, the darkness that had hung heavily just an hour earlier beginning to lift. Knowing she probably wouldn't have another opportunity she pulled out of the parking lot and headed downtown. The one-square-mile village was in a league of its own. There were no streetlights or parking meters and the area had retained a picturesque, old-world feel.

The city regularly hosted delegations from other cities and towns looking to mimic what Carmel-by-the-Sea offered its residents. Every decision the town council made was about retaining the town's character and enhancing its natural coastal beauty. New buildings had to be built around existing trees and new trees had to be planted in areas where they were deemed too meager.

When the town was initially developed, the businesses, cottages and houses had no street numbers. The artisans who built the first homes there had named them instead. Confounding the postal service, residents were unable to receive mail delivery to those individual addresses, instead having to pick up their mail from the post office. The practice continued, the post office becoming a local meeting place of sorts, and everyone seemed to know everyone else by name.

Rebecca had become attached to the town and its community. She had come to understand completely what Nathaniel found so fascinating about it. And although they had only briefly talked about her moving her life, and her business, there, she had doubts that she had yet to profess. She found an empty parking space, shifted her car into Park and disengaged the engine. She sat still for a moment, waiting out another downpour.

Rebecca was still awed by the fact that she was suddenly in a relationship after years of believing that she would never find anyone to love her the way she wanted to be loved. Dating had become a chore. Weeding the good guys from the massive barrel of bad guys had become an art form. Men had far more choices, and unless a woman wanted to be less discerning and settle for mediocrity, finding a good man wasn't as easy as it sounded.

Although she usually told Nathaniel everything, she had not bothered to share half of her dating experiences with her friend. One or two dates had been too painful to recall, not even jokingly. He had fared better with the money-hungry, status-seeking females who yearned to be married to a brilliant surgeon, and that wasn't saying much.

She had tried speed dating, church singles groups, blind dates and online dating. Blind dates had been the absolute worst. She'd lost count of the number of men who had turned around at the door, not even bothering to introduce themselves, turned off that she wasn't a size-two supermodel. Most didn't care to voice what their issues were. Only one had been bold enough to actually call her obese out loud, spitting it out like he was telling her something she didn't know.

Despite the body shaming and sometimes hurtful comments, Rebecca hadn't been fazed. She was comfortable in her skin. She liked her curves. It didn't matter to her if anyone else had an issue. She was big girl magic embodied in a spirited personality and a compassionate heart. She was a great catch. She had money in the bank, owned her own home, ran her own business, and despite the fact she wasn't the greatest cook, she was damn good in bed. Nathaniel had hit the relationship jackpot and the fact that he knew it was icing on some very sweet cake.

Rebecca wasn't sure what she was looking for as she perused the galleries and shops on Ocean Drive. She only knew that she wanted something special to gift to Nathaniel in honor of his newest venture. Something that would show how proud she was of him and how much she loved him. They were just days from the grand opening and although this wasn't her first time looking, she knew that she was quickly running out of time.

Running into Jeffrey Baylor had not been in her plans, but when she exited Nature's Bounty, the gem and mineral store, turning toward Nazar Turkish Imports, the two literally slammed into each other. Jeffrey had not been paying attention, focused on his cell phone. Rebecca had been distracted, trying to decide if she should fly back to LA to find what she was looking for. Neither had seen the other until they'd tripped over each other. Shock and surprise washed over their expressions as Jeffrey reached out to catch her from falling to the ground. The two extended their apologies at the same time and then recognition set in.

"Excuse me!"

"I'm so sorry!"

"Jeffrey! I didn't see you!"

"Rebecca, are you okay? I am so sorry!"

She smiled, her eyes wide. "Well, this takes running into each other to a whole other level." She smoothed her hands down the length of her dress.

"It's all my fault," Jeffrey said, "I should've been paying attention."

"We're both to blame. So, how are you?"

Jeffrey grinned. "I'm well. Better now after seeing your beautiful face."

"You were always the one with the smooth answers, Jeffrey. I see some things haven't changed."

Jeffrey laughed, the deep baritone of his voice resonating warmly through the late afternoon air. "So, what brings you downtown?"

"Just a bit of shopping. Looking for a gift for a friend. What about you?"

"I had to run by the post office to mail out some packages. Then I thought I would run by the candy shop and pick up some fudge. They have really good fudge."

Rebecca laughed. "I see you still have that sweet tooth of yours."

"It seems like it's the only bad habit I can't break."

Jeffrey was staring at her intently and she felt like he was practically undressing her with his eyes. She crossed her arms over her chest, suddenly feeling out of sorts.

She said, "Well, it was good to see you again."

"The last time I saw you, we really didn't get an opportunity to talk before you ran out on me," Jeffrey responded. "If you have a few minutes, maybe we can grab a cup of coffee down at the café?"

Rebecca looked around anxiously, stealing a quick glance at her wristwatch.

"Only if you have a few minutes and you feel comfortable," Jeffrey persisted.

Rebecca hesitated, unsure about whether there was anything either needed to say to the other. Knowing that she really didn't have any reason not to talk to Jeffrey, and Nathaniel wouldn't be back for at least another two hours, she said yes.

"Sure," she said. "I'd love a cup of coffee."

Minutes later they sat across from each other at the Carmel Coffee and Cocoa Bar with two cups of cappuccino and a plate of Danish pastries.

"Are you going to eat all of those pastries?" Rebecca asked.

He laughed. "I was hoping you could help me."

Rebecca shook her head. "No, I'm going to let you

tackle that plate all by yourself." She picked up her coffee cup and took a sip.

"So," Jeffrey started after swallowing a bite of sugared dough and pecans, "why did you run the last time I saw you?"

Rebecca shot him a look. "I didn't run. We really didn't have anything to say to each other so there was no point in my staying."

Jeffrey nodded his head slowly. "I've missed you, Rebecca."

"You really didn't," she responded. "You only think you did."

He chuckled softly. "You never did trust the feelings I had for you, did you?"

"I trusted that you always said what you thought I wanted to hear."

"Are you happy, Rebecca?"

"I'm very happy."

"Even though you don't have a man in your life?"

"Who said I don't have a man?"

Jeffrey's eyebrows lifted in surprise. "I'm sorry. I didn't know you were with someone. I thought…"

"It's a good thing you don't get paid to think," Rebecca interjected.

"Actually, I really don't miss that smart mouth of yours."

"Now, there's the Jeffrey I remember!"

"I wasn't trying to be hurtful, Rebecca. I really wasn't. I had just forgotten how quick you are with the comebacks."

She shrugged and took another sip from her cup.

"So tell me, who's the lucky guy?" He tried to change the subject.

Rebecca met the look he was giving her with one of her own. "Let's talk about you. Last time I heard you were still in Europe. When did you get to Carmel?"

"Actually, my ex-wife brought us here."

"Ex-wife? You've been married?" Rebecca tried not to let the surprise register on her face.

"Four years, before she left me. Her name was Julia and I met her in Paris. We had only known each other for a month when we married. It was not a stellar time for me."

"And Julia just up and left you?"

"After I opened the restaurant she got a case of wanderlust. She didn't want to be here anymore, claims I never had any time for her. She met an artist here named Carlo and they went back to Paris to build his career."

"I'm sorry to hear that. I'm sure that was difficult for you."

"Not really. She was right. I spent more time with my restaurant than I did with her."

Rebecca stared at him, not sure how to respond. Jeffrey didn't wait for her to comment.

"I just knew you and Stallion would have been married with a dozen kids," he said.

"What makes you say that?"

"I offered you Paris and you chose an unemployed medical student. Figured that had to be love."

"Your jealousy for Nathaniel always did get the better of you."

"Jealousy? I was never jealous of him."

"You sure about that? Anytime I mentioned him you got an attitude. If I said he cooked a great pasta, you'd spend the next month trying to outdo his spaghetti. It was too much sometimes. All I wanted back then was for my boyfriend and my best friend to get along. You never even made an effort."

Jeffrey took a deep breath and she could see his jaw tighten in frustration. "Having the woman you love constantly comparing you to her best guy pal wasn't without its challenges. You always choosing him over me didn't help."

An uncomfortable silence descended over the table. Rebecca suddenly took a deep breath, blowing it slowly past her lips. "I'm sorry," she said finally. "It wasn't fair to you and I owe you an apology for putting you in that position."

"Excuse me?"

"I have always been in love with Nathaniel. Even back then. You never had a chance and you deserved better."

"So, are you and he together now?"

Rebecca's smiled drew full and wide across her face. Small hollows dimpled her cheeks. "We are."

"And you're okay with him dating other women?"

"Excuse me?"

"He's dating my friend Elise. She's a real estate agent who…"

"I know who she is."

"And you're okay with him not putting you first?"

"I assure you, there's nothing going on with him and Elise."

Nodding his head slowly, Jeffrey didn't look convinced.

The conversation was suddenly interrupted when someone called Jeffrey's name from across the room. The man approaching their table stood as wide as he was tall, reminding Rebecca of the Macy's Santa Claus. He sported a thick beard and mustache that was the color of freshly fallen snow with a full head of silvery curls to match. The sight of him moved everyone to smile as he played on his jolly personality.

Jeffrey stood to shake his hand. "Dan, my man! How are you?"

Jeffrey's friend responded cheerily as his arm pumped Jeffrey's up and down in greeting. "I'm doing very well. It's good to see you."

"I missed you last month. My staff told me you made the delivery personally."

"I did. I've missed being out on the road. And I owed you a drink. Was hoping I'd be able to pay up." He tossed Rebecca a quick look. "And who might this pretty lady be? Is this why you're never around lately?"

Jeffrey chuckled. "Where are my manners. Rebecca Marks, allow me to introduce you to Dan Weathers. Dan and his family own Liberty Food Services. They're the local distributor for this area. Dan, this is Rebecca."

"The Rebecca I've heard so much about?"

Jeffrey's laugh was nervous as Rebecca rolled her eyes at him. She extended her hand.

"It's very nice to meet you, Mr. Weathers."

"Please, call me Dan. Mr. Weathers was my father and he wasn't quite as handsome as I am."

Rebecca laughed. "I do believe you were on my list of people to call tomorrow."

"Really? Then I am surely a lucky man! To what do I owe the honor?"

"I placed an order with your company that's supposed to be delivered later this week. I was going to follow up to make sure that our delivery was on schedule."

"Who's the delivery?"

"The new restaurant on 17-Mile Drive. The owner is Nathaniel Stallion."

Dan nodded. "I'll make sure to check on it the minute I get back to the office. I'm sure if there were any problems with it, though, you would have heard before now. I wouldn't worry if I were you."

Rebecca smiled. "I wasn't worried," she said, suddenly in need of the restroom. She pushed back her chair and rose from the table. "If you gentlemen would excuse me, please. I need to go powder my nose."

As Rebecca moved across the room, Dan slid into her empty seat. He and Jeffrey stared after her.

"She's even prettier than you said and I do like them thick!"

Jeffrey nodded. "And she is still hung up on Stallion. After all this time he can still do no wrong."

Dan laughed. "Every man crashes and burns at some

time. Some just need a little outside help to move them along. A little push over the edge, so to speak."

Jeffrey's eyes narrowed, his smile disingenuous. "So how can we make that happen?"

As Rebecca moved back toward the two men, they were huddled close together, lost in deep conversation. There was something unsettling about them, the two leaning as if they were plotting a conspiracy. She stopped in her tracks, Santa not looking quite as jolly as he had appeared earlier. And the expression on Jeffrey's face was one she knew well—she'd often caught him wearing it when he'd been miffed over a perceived slight. Instinctively, she knew the two were up to no good. But never in her wildest dreams did she imagine it had anything at all to do with her.

Nathaniel felt he was taking a shortcut when he turned down Ocean Drive to head back to his restaurant. The detour didn't actually take any mileage off his trip. He just enjoyed taking in the sights of the main thoroughfare. At the intersection of Ocean Avenue and Carpenter Street he came to a stop, pausing for his turn to move through the crossroads. He took a second to engage the Bluetooth device in his car, dialing Rebecca's cell phone number. He wasn't sure what to make of it when she didn't answer. It had been the third time in that past hour that he had tried calling to no avail. Rebecca wasn't answering and it was unlike her not to call him back or at least text to let him know she'd gotten his messages.

He was early, Rebecca not expecting him for at least another hour. Business had gone better than expected and he was excited to get back and share the news with her. For a brief moment he thought about stopping at his home to see if she was there, but then he changed his mind, opting to proceed to the restaurant instead.

At the corner of Ocean Avenue and Lincoln Street, as he came to another stop, his eyes were drawn to the front door of the local café. He immediately recognized Jeffrey Baylor standing in conversation with another man. He was surprised when Rebecca stepped out of the building behind them. He watched as she seemed to be bidding them both goodbye. There was a bit of polite conversation, some laughter, and then Jeffrey hugged her warmly. Nathaniel watched as Rebecca hugged him back. Something that felt like jealousy rippled in his midsection. Rebecca shook hands with his friend and then headed toward her car.

Nathaniel suddenly had a long list of questions and no answers. What was she doing with Jeffrey? How come he didn't know they were meeting? Why wasn't she answering her damn phone? More important, why was he suddenly in his feelings about all of it?

The driver in the car behind him blew his horn. The sharp sound startled Nathaniel from the trance he'd fallen into. He looked from his rearview mirror, back to the storefront, and then toward the roadway ahead of him. Easing through the intersection, he didn't wait to see in which direction Rebecca headed. He only knew that in that moment he needed to put as much distance between them as he could. At the next intersection he turned the car around and headed back the way he'd come.

Frustration furrowed Rebecca's brow. She still didn't know what to make of her meeting with Jeffrey or his interaction with his friend Dan. She only knew that she was anxious for Nathaniel to return, having missed him while he'd been gone. Her phone rang, pulling her from her musings. Checking the screen, she suddenly realized she'd missed Nathaniel's calls, having turned off the ringer. Her frustration level rose another ten degrees. She answered the incoming call a split second before the line was disconnected. Her sister greeted her on the other end.

"What are you doing?" Felicia asked, not even bothering to say hello.

"And how are you, sister dear?"

"Yeah, hello. What are you doing?"

"I'm here at the restaurant waiting for Nathaniel. He was supposed to meet me here after he came back from Gilroy. But he's late."

"That's weird."

"What's weird?"

"He called me earlier to ask if I had talked to you. He was worried because you weren't answering your phone. So what were you doing?"

Rebecca blew a soft sigh. "I had coffee with Jeffrey."

"Jeffrey who?"

"Jeffrey Baylor."

"Your ex-boyfriend, Jeffrey Baylor?"

"Yes, he's here in Carmel. He owns a restaurant not far from Nathaniel's restaurant."

"So you were ignoring your current boyfriend to hang out with your old boyfriend? Is that what you're saying?"

"It's not like that. Don't even start. It was more about closure than anything else."

"Closure?"

"Isn't that what I said?"

"What happened with you and Nathaniel on your trip?"

"He told me he loved me."

Felicia laughed. "Well, it's about time! I do hope you said it back?"

"I did, and Felicia, we had the most amazing time! I can't begin to tell you how happy I am." Rebecca spent the next few minutes giving her sister a full account of what had transpired with her and Nathaniel since she'd arrived. Her exuberance was infectious and her sister was thrilled to hear the joy that resonated in Rebecca's voice.

"Good for you!" Felicia exclaimed. "I've been telling you since forever that you two were meant to be together."

"You and everybody else. He and I were both just afraid to take the risk."

"Life is about taking risks. If you spend all your time trying to play it safe, then you'll never live. Not like you're supposed to."

"I get that now. I really do."

"Then you better hang up and call him. Because he sounded slightly frazzled. And he seemed like he was excited about something he wanted to share with you."

"I will. I need to check on him anyway. He should have been here a good while ago."

"You are going to tell him about your date with Jeffrey, aren't you?"

"It wasn't a date!"

"Whatever it was, you do plan to tell him, right? Because I know you, Rebecca," Felicia said.

"What do you mean, you know me? What are you trying to say?"

"That you sometimes don't always tell people things they need to know. That's what I mean."

Rebecca paused before she answered. "Well, since you asked, there really isn't anything to tell. I don't see any reason to make it an issue between Nathaniel and me when it doesn't have to be."

"Why does that sound like it's going to be an issue?"

"Because you like to make things bigger than they need to be."

"Don't say I never gave you any good advice, Rebecca."

"And what advice did you give me?"

"To tell him. Keeping secrets from your man, and I'm assuming he is now your man, is not a good idea!"

Rebecca changed the subject. "It's always a pleasure to talk to you, sister dear. I will see you in a few days. You are coming for the grand opening, aren't you?"

"I would not miss it for anything in this world," Felicia said. "Now go call your man back, please, so he can stop worrying about you."

Rebecca was just about to lock up and head out when Nathaniel came through the door. He looked exhausted, weary from a trip that should only have taken a few hours out of his day. Their gazes met for a split second before he snatched his away.

"Hey," Nathaniel said softly.

"Hey yourself! You finally made it back!" Rebecca chimed. "I was starting to worry." She crossed the room and threw her arms around his neck, kissing him sweetly. "I missed you!"

"I tried to call you. A few times," Nathaniel said. "You must have been busy."

Rebecca smiled. "Sorry about that. I hated that I missed you but I did try to call you back."

"My battery died," he said as he sidestepped out of her embrace. He gave her arm a slight squeeze as he moved from her toward the bar.

There was a moment of pause as Rebecca stared after him. Concern washed over her expression. "Is everything okay?"

Nathaniel nodded. "Yeah, everything is fine. So how did your day go?"

"It was a good day. Ran some errands, did a little shopping, that's about it."

"Nothing else happened?"

Rebecca shook her head. For a split second she thought

about Jeffrey, and then just like that she pushed thoughts of the man away. It was like she'd told her sister—no point in making something out of nothing. "No, nothing else happened."

Nathaniel stood staring at her and then he nodded. "Well, I had a very eventful day. I liked the farm. A lot. The owners are good people and I think we're going to work well together. They have a co-op program much like the one Naomi runs and I signed us up to participate. We'll donate so many hours per month to help work the property in exchange for fresh fruits and vegetables. They're going to be a great resource for the restaurant."

"Wow! Working a farm. That should be interesting."

Nathaniel smiled. "It'll be good for me."

"Just you? Not us?"

He shrugged. "You know what I meant."

There was suddenly an awkward air that billowed like bricks between them. Rebecca wasn't sure if she did know what he meant but she didn't bother to say.

Nathaniel grabbed a bottle of water from the small refrigerator beneath the bar. He moved back to where she was standing. "Elise called me today."

"Elise? What does she want?"

He shook his head. "Nothing. She just called to say hello."

"That means she wants something. Or she's up to something. Elise calling just to say hi means she's plotting. Probably trying to figure out when she can give you a naked lap dance."

"You're exaggerating a bit, aren't you?"

"Probably. But then you know how I feel about Elise."

"Exactly how I feel about Jeffrey."

"Jeffrey?"

"Yeah, you remember Jeffrey, don't you?" His head was tilted slightly as he stared at her.

Rebecca smiled. "Then we don't need to talk about either one of them because they are both inconsequential." She wrapped her arms around his neck and pressed a kiss to his lips. "Let's go home. You can tell me about the rest of your day and then make sweet, sweet love to me."

"And you can tell me about yours."

She shrugged. "You already got the highlights. There's nothing else really to tell. I did talk to my sister and she said to tell you hello, but that's about it."

Nathaniel stiffened slightly, forcing a smile to his face. "I'm exhausted, Bec. It's been a long day. Let's just go home and get some rest."

"Is everything okay?" Rebecca questioned again. "You seem like there's something on your mind."

He shook his head. "No. If there were, I would tell you. I don't keep things from you."

Rebecca watched as he turned, moving his way back toward the door. There was an edge of attitude in his tone that she didn't recognize. And just like that her good mood was like a deflating balloon with air seeping from it.

Chapter 10

Rebecca led the way in her car and Nathaniel followed in his. He had an attitude and he knew it but he couldn't rationalize why Rebecca hadn't said anything about meeting with Jeffrey. Why was she so secretive? What was she hiding and why did she think she needed to? His feelings were hurt and he didn't know how to process that pain. He'd never before thought that Rebecca would keep anything from him. They told each other everything. Or at least he had thought they did. And now, knowing that she didn't tell him everything, he couldn't understand why he was feeling so out of sorts about it.

For the first time he was wishing he hadn't insisted she check out of the hotel and move into the house with him. He needed more time to process it all and he knew that with her there in his space such a thing wouldn't be possible.

His phone rang suddenly, surprising him. The device was connected to the car charger Rebecca had just loaned him, having finally garnered enough power to turn back on.

He answered on the third ring, engaging the Bluetooth so his hands would be free. "Hello?"

Noah Stallion greeted him on the other end. "Hey, little brother, what's cooking?"

Nathaniel smiled. "Not much. Not tonight anyway."

"Sorry to hear that. I just knew you'd be stirring up some trouble, somewhere."

"I wish! Just getting ready for the big day. Everyone's still coming, right?"

"You know we would not miss this for anything in the world."

"I appreciate that," Nathaniel said, his tone devoid of emotion.

"So why do you sound so down? I would have thought you'd be on cloud nine."

"Just a lot on my mind."

"Rebecca?"

"How'd you guess?"

"Aren't women always the source of our problems?" Noah said with a hearty laugh.

Nathaniel chuckled. "I wouldn't say that to Cat if I were you. Speaking of, how is she doing?"

"Morning sickness is kicking her butt and she's not

happy about it so I have to suffer with her. Other than that, she's doing really well. Her obstetrician says the baby is healthy and growing. So, it's all good."

"Do you know yet what you're having? Is the baby a boy or a girl?"

"We don't know yet. It's still too early. But I'm hoping for a girl."

"Really! I thought you'd want a son first."

"No, bro! I remember what it was like with you and Nicholas when you two were little. Natalie was so much easier."

"Until she hit her teens!"

Noah laughed. "There was that! But this time I'll be better prepared for it!"

"You really sound happy. I'm excited for you."

"You don't sound happy. What's going on?"

"I know you didn't call to hear me complain."

"Actually, I called to see how your trip was? How did things go with you and Rebecca? Your sisters were pretty excited for you."

"I was excited. And I have to say thanks to you and Cat again for everything you two did. Flying private certainly has its privileges."

Noah laughed. "It does. I'm glad we could help you out. We really wanted you to impress your girl. Not that she wasn't always impressed!"

Nathaniel sighed. "Does Cat keep things from you?" he suddenly blurted out.

"Things like?"

"Like anything! Do you know everything she does?

Or everyone she sees? Does she have secrets that you don't know about?"

"I'm sure there are some things she doesn't share. Hell, she is a woman!" Noah said with a hearty chuckle. "But, I'd say with reasonable certainty that Cat doesn't hide anything important from me. Why? Did Rebecca keep something important from you?"

"I don't know if it's important or not but she met up with her ex-fiancé this afternoon. I was trying to reach her all day and she wasn't answering her telephone. I had some business in Gilroy and came back earlier than she was expecting me and I just happened to see the two of them walking out of a coffee shop together. I've given her ample opportunity to tell me about it and she hasn't said a word. Now I'm wondering what she was hiding."

"Maybe she's not hiding anything. Maybe there's nothing for her to tell or she doesn't think it's important. Do you think she's interested in this man?"

"No! Not at all! Bec loves me. I know that. I just... well... I don't know. I expected more from her so I'm disappointed. I thought she told me everything. I don't hide anything from her."

"Just ask her. Obviously, it's bothering you, so talk about it. You both are too close to let something like this blow up your relationship. Especially since it took you ten years to figure out you wanted a relationship!"

"I guess."

"I never figured you for the jealous type, little brother!"

"I'm not jealous."

"Yes, you are. You're all up in your feelings because you don't like that some other man might have his eye on your woman. That green-eyed monster has bitten you in the butt and it's holding on for dear life! Don't be jealous. If she's yours, claim her. Let her ex-fiancé and everyone else know she's your woman. Point-blank, period. There's no use in either of you playing games with each other."

"I don't know…"

"What's not to know? Do you love her?"

"Yeah, I love her more than anything. She is my entire world and I'd give up everything for her. I think that's why this is bothering me so much. Like what if she doesn't feel the same way."

"You know her. Better than anybody. You know how she feels about you."

"I guess…"

"Let me tell you what I've learned since being married. Women are temperamental creatures. They can be moody, frustrating and extremely sensitive. We have to tread cautiously with their emotions. And if we do, if they trust us, if they trust our hearts, they will be extremely loyal. When a woman loves you, and you are good to her, she will give you the world and you never have to ask for it."

"Marriage taught you all that?"

"Marriage and our mother. Nolan Perry could do no wrong when our mother trusted him. Even when he wasn't doing right. When he was good to Norris Jean and loving toward her, all she cared about was protecting his name and his reputation. Their love was that powerful right up until the day it wasn't. She loved our father that hard until he didn't have love for her."

"Once again, big brother, you are right."

"Hell, I know that! You have the best big brother in the world."

Nathaniel laughed. "You always did say that."

"I keep waiting for you and that knuckleheaded twin of yours to finally realize it."

Nathaniel smiled into the receiver. "Please, don't tell the girls about this conversation."

Noah laughed with him. "They won't hear it from me. But I wouldn't be surprised if your sisters aren't telling me about it before the week is out. I don't know how they do it but they seem to always know everything."

"And it's so damn annoying!" Nathaniel said, the two men laughing heartily together.

He knew. Rebecca didn't know how, but he knew. Nathaniel knew that she had met with Jeffrey and he also knew that she hadn't told him. She cussed, profanity spilling profusely out of her mouth. Now the something that wasn't supposed to be a big deal had become a monumental problem. She knew she needed to say something, but didn't begin to know where to start and not have it become an even bigger issue between them. Like she was purposely keeping secrets from, or worse, she was lying.

Maybe, she thought, she could throw it in casually

before they crawled into bed. Like, *oh by the way, I forgot to tell you, I saw Jeffrey earlier today*. She was suddenly feeling anxious and unhappy with herself and it irritated her that once again her sister had been right. Felicia was going to have a field day with that one. She cursed again.

The shower door suddenly flew open, Nathaniel standing there in full glory. He eyed her with a perverted smirk across his face. "Is there room for me in here?"

Her eyes skated from the tiled walls to the ceiling and back. "I could probably squeeze all this in to make room," she said as she wiggled her hips from side to side.

Nathaniel laughed as he stepped in beside her, closing the sliding glass door after himself. He pressed his naked body against hers, leaning to kiss her shoulder. "So, what's got you swearing?" he asked as he took the loofah sponge from her hand and began to wash it over her back and shoulders.

"You're pissed at me and it's my fault."

"Who said I'm pissed?"

"I know when you're not happy with me, Nate."

He nodded. "Yeah, you're right. I have an issue."

"You know I saw Jeffrey today and you're angry I didn't tell you." She tossed him a look over her shoulder.

His hand dropped lower, trailing slowly against her hips and ass. "So let's talk about that. Why would you not tell me something like that, Bec?"

"Because it wasn't a big deal. I was downtown and

ran into him coming out of the post office. He asked me to have a cup of coffee and talk. I had a few hours to kill and so I said yes. The conversation was basic at best and then I went to the restaurant to wait for you. That was it and it wasn't important. Or at least I didn't think so. But obviously you did."

Rebecca suddenly gasped as Nathaniel's soapy fingers slid between her butt cheeks. Her body clenched in surprise.

"Sorry about that," he said with a low chuckle and then he slapped her ass, the flesh stinging with heated pleasure.

Rebecca shook her head, holding her breath as the wave of sensation passed.

"Don't get an attitude," he said, still lathering her buttock with one hand, the other snaking around her waist to knead her breast. "Only one of us is allowed to have an attitude per day and I've used up the allotment for the week."

"Well, that's not fair! What if I want to get in my feelings about something before Saturday?"

"Everything is fair in love and war. Isn't that how the saying goes?"

"Who cares about the saying. Why did you get mad? Don't you trust me?"

"Of course I trust you, Bec. I trust you with my life. And more importantly, I trust you with my heart! But I don't trust Jeffrey Baylor. And I know him well enough to know that he is hoping to prey on that soft spot you had for him. He knows how sentimental you can be.

I have no doubts he was hoping to get back into your good graces by making you feel guilty about breaking off your engagement."

"That still doesn't tell me why you were mad at me."

"Because we don't have any secrets. Or at least I didn't think we did. I tell you everything, Bec. And, I'm not going to lie, it hurt my feelings when I thought you didn't."

Struggling to focus on the conversation, Rebecca bit down against her bottom lip. It was becoming harder to stall the rising sensations of pleasure that he was eliciting from her body with his steady ministrations. She took a deep inhale of breath, exhaling it slowly before she spoke. "We don't have any secrets, Nate. And from this point forward I promise that I will never again hold anything back. I swear!" she said as she spun around to face him. She held her hand up to her chest, her index and middle fingers crossed in front of her in jest.

Nathaniel laughed. "Okay, I get it. I don't know why I was being so sensitive. You can trust it won't happen again."

"Actually, I kind of like it that you are jealous."

"Why did it have to be jealousy?"

"Are you saying it wasn't?"

"I'm saying that one reason why we have always been as close as we have been is because we talk about everything. That's more important now than it ever was before. You can't stop talking to me, Bec. Not now," he said emphatically. "You can't keep things from me and you don't get to decide what's important for me to know or not know. I'll decide what's important for me and we will decide together what's important for the two of us. Is that understood?"

Rebecca paused for a split second. She nodded her head. "Damn, that just made me so hot!" she muttered. She pressed her body to his and her lips to his mouth.

The kiss was intense and passionate, tongues dueling for position. The hot water that rained over them was beginning to cool, flowing lukewarm over their heads and shoulders. Rebecca was panting heavily as he suddenly thrust his hand between her legs, fingering her sweet spot like a musician tuning a favored instrument. His touch was gentle, yet firm, his fingers hitting the G-spot and all the others in the alphabet. He had her quivering, perspiration mingling sweetly with the water from the showerhead.

Hands danced over flesh, kneading, caressing, teasing. Rebecca reached for the bulge of hardened flesh that he ground brazenly against her leg. She stroked him boldly, clasping his erection tightly in the palm of her hands. The heat from her fingers further ignited the already simmering embers deep in the core of his manhood. He was engorged, his male member tight and full and ready to explode from the pleasure of her touch.

They were both on sensory overload and the moment was suddenly surreal. Nathaniel dropped to his knees and lifted her leg over his shoulder. He kissed her intimately, his tongue like a piston as it darted in and out of her most private place. Rebecca grabbed the back of his head with one hand and the shower rail with the other, holding on for dear life as she pushed and pulled herself against his face. When she orgasmed her body quaked, every muscle quivering and then Nathaniel slid himself into her, riding the waves of her pleasure until he reached his own.

Hours later they lay snuggled against each other in Nathaniel's bed. They'd taken their loving from the shower to the bedroom floor, down the length of hallway toward the kitchen, then back to the bedroom and finally the bed. They were spent and comfortable, emotions feeling in balance once again. The moment was everything either could have ever imagined and it was so much more.

Nathaniel dozed off and on, completely satiated. He lay on his stomach, his body curled slightly against hers, one leg thrown over her backside. One hand gently stroked her flesh, fingers lightly grazing her skin. The other was curled up and over his head, his fingers playing with the length of her hair. He dozed and stroked, then dozed again never breaking the connection between them.

"I'm sorry," Rebecca suddenly whispered into the late night air.

Nathaniel muttered, his words incoherent as sleep pulled at him harder. He squeezed her again.

"I never meant to hurt your feelings," she said softly. And then she, too, fell into a deep sleep.

Chapter 11

They were a good twenty-four hours from the grand opening of Dinner. Nathaniel's restaurant venture was about to be realized. He stood in the center of the dining room taking it all in. With the furniture and decor in place, it was a spectacular sight to behold. The entire space felt welcoming and comfortable and he held out hope that future patrons would feel very much at home there.

For the past two days Rebecca had been bellowing orders like a military general. The two hostesses and the wait staff hired were well prepared, having spent the entire last week learning the ins and out of their kitchen. Nathaniel instinctively knew that one, maybe two, of them wouldn't last through the end of the year but he was good with that. All he asked was that while they were there to work, they gave him their very best effort. Rebecca had threatened a few of them with their lives and even though they had all laughed it off as a joke he knew she was determined to ensure nothing could possibly go wrong. No matter what it took.

In the other room she and the chef that he had hired were in deep conversation. Lorenzo Mackie was fresh out of cooking school. He'd had substantial practice as a sous chef during a six-year stint in prison for robbing a convenience store. After his release, the young man had worked three jobs to put himself through culinary school, graduating at the top of his class from L'école Culinaire. Nathaniel had been impressed with his fortitude. Coming from nothing, Lorenzo been determined to change his life around and do better. He also wanted to buy his mother a house and that alone had helped win him the job twenty-six others had interviewed for.

When Rebecca suddenly came through the swinging doors, her cell phone clutched to her ear, Nathaniel sensed something was wrong. The chef followed on her heels. Lorenzo shot him a look and shook his head.

"What's wrong?" he questioned, looking from her to Lorenzo and back.

Lorenzo shrugged, shoulders pushing skyward as his arms hung down to his sides, his palms facing forward. "We didn't get our order from Liberty. It was supposed to have been here yesterday. When I called they said Rebecca canceled it."

Nathaniel suddenly tensed, his eyes shifting in her

direction. She was in heated conversation with whomever was on the other end and she clearly wasn't happy.

"That is totally unacceptable!" she snapped. "Tell Mr. Weathers to call me and if I don't hear from him today there will be hell to pay!" She disconnected the line and then she swore loudly, a long stream of profanity spewing into the warm afternoon air.

"Yo, sailor! You've been doing that a lot lately," Nathaniel said, moving to her side. "And that potty mouth really doesn't become you."

She cursed again, not easily moved from the anger that pricked her spirit.

"Okay, so what's wrong?" he asked again. "Where's our delivery?"

"According to their dispatcher, I called two days ago to cancel the order. Now, they're saying they can't get what we need until next week. But I did not cancel that order!"

Nathaniel heaved a deep sigh. "Have you called any other suppliers? They can't have the monopoly around here."

"You had very specific items on your order list. The lamb. The red snapper, plus all the basics you needed to simply stock your kitchen. There's stuff on the list Liberty doesn't stock in their warehouse here. They bring it in from their suppliers as needed."

"I placed some calls and no one I talked to can get us what we need by tomorrow," Lorenzo interjected. "And I've called everyone between Seattle and San Diego."

"So we're screwed," Nathaniel said as he pulled his

hands along the side of his head. He bent forward at the waist and gasped. "We're about to have a grand opening with no grand opening food! We are royally screwed."

"Not on my watch," Rebecca spat.

Nathaniel threw up his hands in frustration. "I can appreciate you wanting to make this happen but if we can't...we can't!"

"Maybe we should postpone until next week?" Lorenzo offered, looking from one to the other.

"It's probably for the best," Nathaniel muttered.

"That's not an option," Rebecca snapped.

"Let's be realistic, Bec. We need to start preparing no later than eight o'clock tomorrow morning. There's no way we can make this happen. I need to start making calls. People are planning to travel. There's just..." He suddenly paused, air catching deep in his chest. A flash of rage suddenly crossed his face, the wealth of it simmering in his dark eyes.

Across the room Dan Weathers stood in the doorway, his nonchalant expression feeling out of place. Nathaniel recognized him from when he'd been on the corner, standing with Jeffrey Baylor and Rebecca. Instinctively, his radar darted into the red and he felt his whole body tense.

Dan greeted them cheerily. "Rebecca, I heard you were trying to reach me," he said, crossing the room to where they stood. He extended his hand toward Nathaniel. "You must be Mr. Stallion. I'm so sorry we have to meet under these circumstances. I'm Dan Weathers, one of the owners of Liberty Food Services."

"It's Dr. Stallion," Rebecca corrected. She took a step toward the man. "Can you please explain how our order was canceled? Your secretary claims that you told her I canceled it."

"You did!" Dan said, feigning confusion. "When we met at the coffee shop the other day with your fiancé."

Rebecca bristled. "My fiancé?"

He nodded his head. "Jeffrey Baylor. And I was so excited to meet you. Jeffrey talked about you all the time so I was thrilled when you two were able to re-unite."

"Firstly, Jeffrey is not my fiancé."

"Your boyfriend then."

"He's not my friend, boy or otherwise."

"I'm sorry. I guess I misunderstood."

"Clearly," Rebecca snarled between clenched teeth, "you misunderstood a few things. We never talked about the order you had for this establishment. Never!"

"Didn't we?"

She took another quick step in his direction. Nathaniel reached out and grabbed her by the wrist. Her hands were clenched in tight fists and his touch halted her step. She came to an abrupt stop and took a deep breath. "No, we did not," she snapped.

Dan shook his head from side to side. "I am so sorry then. It was probably the order for Jeffrey's restaurant that should have been canceled. I don't know how I got that wrong!" The man's expression was telling, amuse-ment dancing in his eyes as he feigned ignorance. The absurdity of it all would have actually been funny if it wasn't so egregious.

It suddenly became clear to her. Jeffrey had enlisted his friend to sabotage Nathaniel's grand opening. To undermine her and the hard work they had both invested in the success of his business. Jeffrey had been all kinds of petty and Rebecca found herself dead center of the hurt it was causing Nathaniel. She was suddenly even more pissed than she had been.

Nathaniel suddenly stepped between the two, stalling the punch she was mere seconds from throwing.

"The question, Mr. Weathers, is how you can help make this error of yours right?"

"We will gladly fill your order and give you a fifteen percent discount for the inconvenience. Unfortunately, we won't be able to fill your order until our trucks come in next week. Maybe not even until the week after."

"Twenty-five percent," Rebecca countered as she pulled her hand from Nathaniel's grasp.

"I don't…" Dan started.

"Twenty-five percent on our orders for the next six months or we'll take our business elsewhere."

The man bristled, his cheeks deepening to a bright red beneath his snow-white beard. "That's ridiculous! There's no way I can agree to that."

"Thirty percent or we'll let all of your clients know how you do business and refer them to the supplier who's going to make good on what you screwed up. Thirty percent on all of our orders for the next six months or you'll lose our business and no less than sixty percent of your current client base. And I'll negotiate their rates personally to insure they get a better deal and better service than they have ever gotten from you," she said. "Thirty percent or I will work tirelessly to ruin your good family name and bring Liberty Foods to a semblance of what you are now and I promise there is nothing your good buddy and pal Jeffrey is going to be able to do to help you."

Dan was suddenly stammering. "Maybe twenty-five..."

"Thirty and piss me off a minute longer and it'll be forty-five. I have no doubt that will eat up any profit you might still be getting."

"I need to think about..."

Rebecca dialed. She was staring Dan down as she waited for her call to be answered. "Lisa! How are you? It's Rebecca Marks." She paused as the other woman greeted her. "I just wanted to say thank you. I got your message and I really appreciate the information." There was another pause as Rebecca listened. "Actually, I'm very disappointed in Liberty but I don't want to talk badly about them. One bad apple in the bunch doesn't mean the whole company is spoiled." Pause. "Really? I hadn't heard that. Well, to be honest, I don't know if we'll be using them much longer. They really aren't the only game in town. I've found a wonderful new resource with lower pricing and better product." Pause. "I'll text you the information the minute we hang up and you can tell them I referred you. It'll get you a ten-percent discount on their introductory pricing!"

She paused one last time. "Wonderful! We must do lunch soon! Take care!"

Rebecca disconnected the line, her eyes still locked on Dan's face. She smiled as she narrowed her gaze on him. "That was Lisa Rodelo. She owns the Buy-The-Bull Steak franchise. I think you supply some twenty of their stores from here to LA. She and I are sorority sisters. I also know Camille Gates and her husband Jarrod of Gates Fast Foods. They're some ninety-three stores if I'm correct. And this is only where I'm starting. The food industry is actually a very small world, Dan. There are only six degrees of separation before I blow your little business to high hell."

"Fine," Dan quipped. "Thirty…"

Rebecca held up her index finger, stalling his comment.

"Forty-five. You took too damn long. Make Jeffrey compensate you for the difference. That's what friends are for," she said.

"Jeffrey said you were an icy bitch!" Dan snarled.

"What did you just call her?" Nathaniel said, his head tilted ever so slightly.

"You heard me…" Dan started, and then Nathaniel nailed him, punching him so hard he landed on the floor with a resounding thud.

"Aww, snap!" Lorenzo chimed.

Nathaniel shook his hand, wincing from the hurt of it. "So, now we have no food and I'll probably go to jail for assault," he said, tossing a look toward Rebecca.

She grinned, her mind already racing to figure out

how she was going to fix the possibility of someone calling the police on Nathaniel. She made a mental note to call the attorney he kept on retainer the first free minute she had. "That's not going to happen today, either. You have a grand opening tomorrow. I'll call one of our legal friends and get them to contact the station and promise you'll turn yourself in first thing Monday after you get back into town or something," she said, already getting his story in order.

Nathaniel rolled his eyes skyward, not wanting to fathom what she might have up her sleeves. He changed the subject back to food. "And, you really do have someone else you think can supply us?"

"Not yet, but he didn't need to know that."

Nathaniel shook his head. "I can't with you right now, Bec. I need some air," he said and then exited the building, leaving them all behind.

Lorenzo tossed her a look. "You want me to put ole' boy in his truck?"

"You would do that?" Rebecca asked.

"I don't think you want him coming to right here in the middle of the restaurant. I'm just going to help him outside. Hopefully when he wakes up he won't remember anything."

Rebecca laughed, a nervous titter that served to ease her anxiety. "Thank you," she said, and then, "when you're done, I could use your help with something else."

Lorenzo grinned. "Whatever you need, boss lady. You've got gumption! Reminds me of my mother and she could outwit the sleaziest snake-oil salesman!"

"I think I'm really going to like your mother."

Dan suddenly groaned, a leg flailing slightly.

"Let me take out the trash," Lorenzo said as he lifted the Santa look-alike with relative ease and slung him over his shoulders. "Then I'll be right back to help you and Dr. Stallion with whatever you need!"

Rebecca had always talked a good game, Nathaniel mused. Her negotiating skills were top in their league and she could impressively hold her own against the best in most businesses. In that moment, though, he didn't know what to believe. Rebecca had asked him to trust her and be assured that she could get what they needed in time for his grand opening. Everything pointed to that being near impossible, yet something had him more than willing to lay all his bets on her. He couldn't help but wonder, though, if he too had completely lost his mind.

He sat in the sand, staring out toward the ocean. After his encounter with Dan Weathers he had come home. Home had made the most sense as he waited to see if Jeffrey's partner in crime was going to press charges against him. He had made one other stop before reaching his front door. Slamming his fist into Jeffrey Baylor's face had only seemed fitting. He figured there was no reason to waste a good arrest. If they were going to lock him up, they may as well lock him up for both crimes.

Jeffrey had greeted him with a sarcastic comment and that had been all it took. As Jeffrey had struggled to get back up on his feet, Nathaniel had admonished him to stay clear of Rebecca, threatening him with worse if he were to ever try to get near her again. He'd borrowed a few choice words from Rebecca's vocabulary, cursing the man as he exited the room.

Now, sitting in reflection on the beach that bordered his backyard, he couldn't help but wonder if maybe he'd made a mistake. He heard her calling his name and looked up to see Rebecca sauntering in his direction. There was just enough sway in her hips as she stomped toward him that moved him to smile. *How did I get so lucky?* he mused. *What have I done to be blessed so abundantly?*

"Where is your phone?" she questioned as she reached his side and dropped down to the sand beside him.

He shrugged. "In the house. I didn't have any need for it."

"I beg to differ. You weren't answering my call and I was starting to worry. If you'd had your phone, you would've saved me a trip."

"Sorry." His tone was hardly convincing as he leaned back on his elbows.

Rebecca skewed her face in frustration. "Aren't you going to ask me about your delivery?"

"Nope."

"Or about Dan Weathers?"

Nathaniel shook his head, his disinterest feeling almost corporeal.

"Nothing? You're not going to ask me anything?"

"I said no, Bec! I really don't give a damn!"

"Oh, yes, you do!"

"No, I don't. I'm not really not concerned about any of it. You said there will be food stuffs ready and waiting for me when I reach the kitchen tomorrow morning. You also said I won't get arrested tonight or tomorrow. And I'm going to trust that you know what you're talking about while I sit here and watch the sun set."

"Are you okay?"

"Actually, I feel fine."

"You're scaring me, Nate."

Nathaniel laughed. "Why? I would think that you would be celebrating the fact that I'm not agonizing over the situation."

"That's why you're scaring me. This ain't like you."

"No, it's not." There was a moment of hesitation as Nathaniel seemed to slip into thought. You could almost see his mind racing as he searched for the words to explain himself. He reached for her hand and held it, his fingers intertwined with hers.

"When I was a little boy I use to worry about everything. We went through some really hard times. For the longest time, it felt like my mother was always angry about something. It wasn't until I was an adult that I understood that she was just sad all the time. But I worried about her. I worried about Nicholas and Natalie because they were the youngest. I worried about whether we would eat. I worried when we didn't have friends. I worried about never having a father. You name it and I'm sure I worried about it! I worried because it was all I could do and I worried because it felt like my twin never worried about anything."

There was a moment of pause as Nathaniel fell into thought, seeming to need a moment to collect his thoughts. He took a breath before continuing.

"You know what I went through when Nicholas had his accident. I think you know better than anyone else how much that tormented me. All I did was worry. I worried about his medical care. I worried about his relationships. I worried about his future. I drove myself crazy constantly worrying about things I couldn't control.

"What I know and what I have finally become reconciled to is that all we can do is accept the hand we've been dealt. To live our lives to the fullest, no matter what cards are handed to us. I am just tired of worrying about everything, Bec! I wasted too many years worrying about you and me and what might happen if we were ever to be in a relationship. And now that we are, I am happier than I have ever been.

"But what I have never worried about is you being able to do something you set your mind on accomplishing. You, Bec, I have always trusted, emphatically! And, because you say that I will have a grand opening tomorrow, I am going to sit my happy ass right here in this sand and watch the sunset. Then I'm going to take you into the house and make love to you. I am going to love you until my body fails me or you beg me to stop! Whichever comes first. Then I'm going to get a good night's sleep so that when my alarm goes off at five-thirty in the morning I can get up and get to work without it being a problem. Any other questions?"

Rebecca grinned. "No, sir. Sounds like you have a plan. Let go and let God!"

"No," he said firmly. "Let go and *trust* God. It's probably the one thing in my life that I have never done honestly."

Rebecca blinked away the tears that suddenly pressed hot behind her eyelids. Nathaniel wrapped his arms around her and pulled her close. With nothing else to say, they slipped into a quiet reverie, watching as the bright sun settled into the recesses of cumulus clouds that filled the sky and kissed the coastline of water in the distance.

Chapter 12

Nathaniel never asked her what she had done, or even if, she had been able to secure the food stocks they needed. He didn't ask and she saw no reason to volunteer the information. Most especially since he had yet to volunteer that he had gone to see Jeffrey Baylor, leaving the man with a broken nose and busted lip. Holding that over his head one day would come in handy, most especially if she somehow managed to forget to tell him something he suddenly deemed important.

It hadn't been easy to ensure that the walk-in refrigerator and food stores were completely stocked with everything he needed. In fact, hours of cold calling had left her doubtful and teary-eyed. With every viable resource coming to a dead end, Rebecca had begun to lose hope, but hope hadn't given up on her.

Lorenzo had reached out to a former inmate and friend who had suggested they try venues that often catered to last-minute demands for those willing to pay the price. He'd given him the name of a sous chef at the Bellagio Hotel in Las Vegas. That sous chef was no longer employed by the hotel and they were transferred to the head chef who was unable or unwilling to take their call.

Not to be deterred, Rebecca went through her list of sorority sisters, seeking help. It was Catherine Moore-Stallion, an Alpha Kappa Alpha sister, who pointed her to Nathaniel's cousin John Stallion, owner of the Boudreaux hotel empire. The staff at Stallion Enterprises had sent her a list of suppliers, but also directed her to the hotel chain's original owner Mason Boudreaux. Mason had been delighted to offer his assistance, calling one of his personal contacts directly.

A private delivery service had gotten the entire order onto a Fly-High Dot Com jet, the Stallion family's personal aircraft landing at the Monterey Peninsula Airport shortly after one o'clock in the morning. Lorenzo, with help from Nathaniel's brother, sisters and cousins, had gotten everything from the airport to the restaurant with no major speed bumps. Lorenzo had kept her abreast along the way, finally wishing her one last goodnight when everything was in its place in the kitchen. She didn't begin to know how to show her appreciation, but insisting Nathaniel give the man a raise was at the top of her list.

Never once did she let on how frightened she was that she couldn't make it happen. She kept her doubts and fears to herself, seeing no reason to cause Nathaniel an ounce of concern. After reading Lorenzo's final text message she blew a sigh of relief. Those six degrees of separation that could have torn a business down had helped to build one instead.

Rolling over, she kissed Nathaniel passionately. She lifted her body above his, teasing him with a slow rotation of her hips. Nathaniel smiled.

"I didn't wave that white flag yet," Rebecca whispered softly.

Nathaniel met her gyrations with his own. He clutched her hips and pulled her against himself. "My body hasn't failed me yet," he said with a wide grin.

She plunged her body down against the protrusion of flesh that stood at attention between them. "I've got this," she said. "You just lay on back and let me ride!"

Nathaniel chuckled. "You don't have to tempt this Stallion twice!"

From the moment Nathaniel stepped through the doors of Dinner he felt a monumental energy through the space. It was all hands on deck as they began to prepare for their very first meal. Lorenzo was there to greet him at the door, excited to guide him through the pantries and the refrigerators as they pulled ingredients to the counters to cook.

Rebecca stood in the entrance to the kitchen and watched him. Nathaniel was in his element, and there was an air of calm that had settled around his shoulders like a much beloved blanket. Seeing him filled with such emotion tugged at her heartstrings, twisted them in a tight knot and filled her with infinite joy. In that moment she didn't know it was possible to love anyone as much as she loved him. Her love for Nathaniel was abundant beyond measure.

The aroma through the kitchen was decadent. The scent of fresh vegetables and marinating meat teased her hunger pangs. She'd had to pull him away in the middle of the afternoon to do an interview with the local newspaper. There was no missing the excitement in his voice. His enthusiasm about the food preparation and what he had planned for the inaugural meal was contagious. Even the reporter, a journalism student on break from her junior year at West Valley College in Saratoga, was excited for the ribbon-cutting.

Shortly before four-thirty Rebecca ensured that all of the wait staff on duty were prepared and ready. It would only be another hour before the doors were scheduled to open. Behind the locked door of his office she implored him to grab a quick shower and change.

"Everything in the kitchen is fine!" she exclaimed. "Lorenzo has it all under control."

"Lorenzo has been a godsend," Nathaniel said. "I foresee big things in his future."

"I agree. He's good people."

Heading into his private bathroom, Nathaniel took

a moment to himself to relax. Rebecca had insisted on the space during the renovations, offering a viable argument why it was necessary. He was glad he'd given in despite his initial efforts to sway her from it. She'd persisted through, insisting it would save time when he needed to change quickly.

He grabbed a quick shower, shaved away the first hint of new beard growth and slipped on the casual suit that Rebecca had picked out for him. The gray silk fit his frame nicely and paired over a white dress shirt with a vibrant red pocket hankie he looked quite dashing. With one last glance in the mirror he moved back into the office area. Rebecca sat waiting, prayers whispered skyward as she sought one more favor from God.

Nathaniel smiled. "What did you pray for?"

"Just wanted to say thank-you," she answered. "Besides, I've made so many deals with God, I doubt that He even listens to me anymore."

"Oh, He listens," Nathaniel teased. "And I've told you about making promises you can't keep."

"Oh, I've kept them. I've kept them all and you know me well enough to know that wasn't always easy."

Nathaniel moved around the desk. He pulled open the top drawer. Inside, a small gift box rested beneath a stash of papers. Pulling it into his hands he moved back to where Rebecca was standing.

"I've thought about how to do this a million times," Nathaniel said.

Rebecca's eyes widened. "How to do what? What are you doing?"

He smiled at her, tossing her a teasing look. "How to come full circle."

She shook her head. "I don't understand."

"How to celebrate my life coming full circle by asking my best friend to be my wife *and* my best friend."

Nathaniel dropped down onto one knee. He flipped the lid on the small box and exposed a brilliant four-carat diamond ring. The styling was simple, with a gold band that had been engraved with both their initials and the date. "Rebecca Marks, will you marry me?"

Tears misted Rebecca's eyes. She tried to contain her exuberance, fighting not to jumping up and down with excitement. "Yes, yes, yes, yes, yes!"

Her hand shook as Nathaniel slid the ring onto her finger. He kissed the back of her hand and rose back to his feet and kissed her mouth. Rebecca pressed her palms to the side of his face, her lips gliding against his with ease. Everything about the moment was sweeter than imagined, a young girl's fairy tale come true.

"You smell like first-time sex," Nathaniel whispered into her ear. "If we had the time I'd lay you across this desk and make love to you."

Rebecca giggled. "First-time sex? As opposed to second, third or fourth time?"

"Like the first time I inhaled you and you made me hard! Like it feels every time I touch you! Like it's the first time and I'm about to discover something else new and beautiful about you."

Rebecca reached her arms around his neck and kissed him intently. When they finally pulled from each other, coming up for air, she smiled. "Don't you have some work to do?"

He nodded. "You better believe it, baby!"

Hand in hand the two exited the office space, wide grins filling their faces. He looked around the room and nodded his approval. A quick pep talk to encourage his staff energized them all and after checking the kitchen one last time, Nathaniel was ready to open the doors.

Family and friends filled the restaurant's private dining room. Rebecca sat in conversation with Nathaniel's sister Naomi and her new husband Patrick O'Brien. Their sister Natalie sat across the table from her, chatting with Carl Parker and two men from his construction crew who had worked on the renovations. Noah and Nicholas were huddled together in the corner of the room, conversing with their cousins John and Mark Stallion out of Texas. John and Mark's wives, as well as their siblings, their siblings' spouses and their children, were all in attendance. It was one huge family reunion with extended family that included the entire Boudreaux clan out of New Orleans that two of the Stallion siblings and Nathaniel's twin Nicholas had married into.

There had been an official ribbon-cutting ceremony to kick things off. The mayor and four city council members had shown for the promotional opportunity. It was an election year and each of them was at risk of losing his or her position. Nathaniel had taken the opportunity to thank his contractor and the work crews for all of their efforts. Carl had waved his hands excitedly, his chest pushed forward like a proud peacock. Nathaniel had acknowledged Lorenzo's culinary skills, expressing his excitement at working alongside the man. He thanked his family, naming each of the siblings individually as he offered brief anecdotes about something that was special between them. He'd even given a shout-out to his father and half siblings who'd come to show their support. Before closing out the speeches he had expressed his gratitude for everything Rebecca had done since coming to be by his side. The entire thirteen minutes and twenty-three seconds had been emotional and heartwarming.

A crowd still lingered in the main dining room, having turned over at least two times that Rebecca knew of. Dinner was quickly becoming the talk of the town. Rebecca sensed that Nathaniel's unique approach to family dining would soon become a fan favorite.

Large banquet tables adorned the space, offering communal, family-style dining. Food was served on platters and in large bowls brought to the table for guests to pass around and serve themselves. The serving dishes were left on the table and replenished as needed by the wait staff. It was a personal, intimate dining experience enjoyed by all.

Nathaniel planned for the menu to change noticeably week to week and completely month to month. The grand opening fare was a mélange of his favorites and hers. There was sweet potato ravioli with a fresh garden sage and brown butter sauce, arugula salad with baby cut greens, Italian-cut sirloin steak with roasted garlic and rosemary, red snapper with a basil dressing, and freshly roasted tomatoes with a basil chiffonade. Baskets of rosemary focaccia bread sat on the center of each table and the dessert menu included limoncello ricotta cheesecake with roasted figs and coffee-infused tiramisu. It was a feast of the freshest vegetables, prime-cut meats and meticulously balanced flavors. Even the most discerning palates enjoyed the meal and everyone ate well.

Looking around the room, Nathaniel was in awe of the crowd who had shown up to support him. All of his family, his fraternity brothers, medical colleagues and those who he loved most were all there. He'd gotten emotional about it a few times, fighting not to let it show on his face. The many expressions of love and encouragement just further solidified his belief that he'd made the right choice.

He hurried from the dining room back to the kitchen to double-check once again that all was well. Before he returned he stopped at each table to personally greet the paying customers and welcome them to his culinary world. There were glowing reviews and everyone seemed to be enjoying themselves immensely. If he hadn't known prior to opening, he was definitely certain after the last meal had been plated that he had a winning formula on his hand.

As he moved back into the private dining room Rebecca was being accosted by two little girls. It suddenly dawned on him that warning Rebecca about some of his family might have been a good idea. Eleven-year-old Gabrielle Stallion, the daughter of his cousin John and his wife Marah, stood on one side poking Rebecca in the chest. Fourteen-year-old Irene Stallion, the daughter of his cousin Mark and his wife Michelle, stood on the other side with her arms crossed, her expression voicing annoyance and disinterest. He could only begin to imagine the conversation being held between them. Clearly, the dynamic duo didn't know they had just met their match. He eased his way over so he could eavesdrop on what was proving to be a titillating conversation.

"But you have really big breasts," little Gabi was saying. "I mean *really* big!"

"Little girl if you poke me one more time," Rebecca said, narrowing her gaze on the child, "I will hurt you. And they're not that big!" she snapped.

Gabi seemed unfazed as she poked Rebecca one last time to emphasize her point. "Irene wants big breasts. She wears a bra now. But it's a small bra. Auntie Mitch said that it's a training bra, but Irene doesn't have no breasts to teach. She might get 'em soon though!"

Dismay washed over Irene's little face. She was trying to maintain her composure but everyone watching could tell she was just seconds away from punching her favorite cousin in the face. "I have breasts and my mommy says they're still growing," Irene said matter-of-factly. "You're the one who doesn't have breasts!"

Mark Stallion suddenly intervened. "Why are you two talking about your boobs again? I thought we had a conversation about things that were appropriate to talk about in public and things your fathers don't want to hear!"

"It wasn't me, Daddy," Irene chimed. "Gabi still acts like a little baby."

"I do not!" Gabi said as she poked Rebecca on the other side for good measure.

"Somebody come get their children," Rebecca admonished loudly. "Before I make them shorter than they already are!"

Everyone in the room laughed heartily.

Michelle Stallion gestured for her daughter's attention. "Irene, why are you bothering people? And what have I told you about keeping your hands to yourself?"

"I didn't do anything!" Irene whined. "It was all Gabi!"

"It was all Gabi," Marah Stallion interjected, her head bobbing against her neck. "It's always Gabi."

Another round of laughter filled the room.

"You two come sit down over here with me," Mark chastised. "We told you both about behaving and it didn't take you ten minutes to get into trouble."

Both girls stomped off after him, pouting profusely.

"I am so sorry!" Marah intoned. "She's getting better but we're not quite there yet. She can still be quite a handful."

"It's all good," Rebecca said as she winked her eye. "I was actually enjoying our conversation until she started poking my boob." Rebecca rubbed at the offending bruise.

"They're both suddenly fascinated with wanting

breasts! One insisted on a bra even though she doesn't need one yet and the other keeps asking so she can keep up with the big girls."

"It's driving John and Mark crazy!" Michelle said with a deep laugh.

"Are they your only ones?" Rebecca asked as she looked around the room.

Both women answered at the same time. "Yes, thank goodness!"

Rebecca laughed, amusement dancing over her face.

"Are you looking forward to having children, Rebecca?" Tarah Boudreaux Stallion asked joining in the conversation.

"To be honest, the thought scares the hell out of me!" Rebecca responded.

The young neurosurgeon nodded. "Nicholas and I feel the same way!"

"I know exactly how you feel," Catherine Moore-Stallion interjected. She rubbed her palm against the newly blossoming rise of her pregnant belly. "There's no going back now, though," she added.

Naomi wrapped her sister-in-law in a warm embrace. "No worries, Cat! We're so excited for you that you don't need to worry about a thing."

"I know that's right," Natalie said. "I may even leave Paris to come home for this new baby."

"Well!" Noah exclaimed. "We might have ten babies if it means you'll come home."

"You might have ten babies," Cat said with a deep

laugh. "I need to have the first one before we even think about talking about more."

Noah laughed with his wife. "I'm banking on us being as fertile as Dahlia and Guy," he said, pointing to the Boudreaux side of their family. They had five children—two sets of twins and one single birth—and a host of nannies to give the busy film director and movie star a helping hand.

A shrill scream suddenly resounded from the other side of the room. Rebecca's sister jumped from her seat and came rushing to Rebecca's side. She grabbed her sister's hand and waved it in the air. "Is that what I think it is?" Felicia questioned, looking from Rebecca to Nathaniel and back.

A rush of color suddenly flooded Rebecca's face, tinting her cheeks a deep shade of red. She was suddenly acutely aware of the whole family staring at her. From where he stood Nathaniel laughed heartily. He raised his hand in the air for everyone's attention and the room fell mildly quiet, just the chatter of the underage crowd making noise.

"First, I want to thank you all again for showing up to support me. I can't begin to tell you how much it means to me."

He circled his way around the table and moved to Rebecca's side, resting his hands against her shoulders. "You are all very important to me, which is why I'm even more excited to share that right before opening the doors this evening, I asked Rebecca to be my wife and she said yes!" He leaned to kiss her lips.

The room erupted in cheers and applause. Felicia hugged her sister, tears streaming down both their faces. She punched Nathaniel playfully in the arm, then leaned to give her future brother-in-law a hug.

Chapter 13

After the doors at Dinner were closed and locked, the party moved to Nathaniel's home. Most of the children had fallen asleep, sprawled across the beds in the spare bedrooms. Down on the private beach the men had built a large bonfire. It blazed beautifully against the backdrop of the ocean waters.

The couples were all huddled together, wrapped around each other, sitting atop every blanket Rebecca had been able to find in Nathaniel's linen closets. They'd also carried down the few aluminum folding chairs that usually rested on his back deck. Nathaniel had hustled up marshmallows, graham crackers and some very expensive chocolate bars for s'mores. The last bottles of wine and champagne from dinner and the beer Nathaniel had in his fridge flowed like water between them. Someone had called it a family-friendly orgy and an abundance of laughter rang warmly through the late-night air.

Rebecca rested her tired torso against Nathaniel's broad chest. His arms were wrapped lovingly around her, his fingers brushing gentle caresses against the backs of her hands and her forearms. Occasionally, he would knead the flesh of her upper thighs or the small tire of cushion around her midsection. His touch was loving and easy, bringing her an air of comfort that she found immensely heartwarming.

She'd been lost in her own thoughts when someone calling Nathaniel's name pulled her back to the conversation. She looked up as the Boudreaux family patriarch, Senior Boudreaux, leaned in their direction.

"Son," Senior started, "your father was just telling me how proud he is of you. And, I wanted to say the same. It makes me and my Katherine very proud, when we see you young people reaching for your dreams and finding great success. I have no doubt you have worked very hard to make every one of your late mother's dreams for you come true."

"Thank you, sir," Nathaniel replied. "I greatly appreciate you saying that."

Rebecca knew Nathaniel had great respect for the patriarch. He had often mused what it might have been like had his own father been there for him the way Senior had been there for his children.

Nolan Perry, Nathaniel's biological father, sat on the

other side beside Katherine Boudreaux. His father gave him a slight salute and winked his eye to affirm what the other man had said. Nathaniel appreciated the gesture, most especially since they were still working toward building their father-son relationship.

A short while later Rebecca went inside to search out the beer nuts and pretzels she knew to be hidden on a top shelf in the pantry. When she'd reached the patio landing and disappeared into the home, Noah assumed the seat she'd just vacated. The two men exchanged a dap, a handshake of sorts where they bumped fists.

"I just wanted to say something to you before we headed back to Utah and it left my mind," Noah said.

"What's up?" Nathaniel asked. He took a sip from the bottle of beer in his hands.

"I just thought you might like to know that we are all extremely impressed with Rebecca. She's one hell of woman and you are a very lucky man."

"Thank you," Nathaniel responded. "I really appreciate that."

"Really, it's very important to all of us, me, the girls and especially Nicholas, that you've found someone so special to share your life with."

"Did I miss something? It's not like she was a stranger to you all. I thought you guys had always been impressed with her?"

"We were. We have liked Rebecca since day one. But what she did for you in the last twenty-four hours was nothing short of miraculous. I was genuinely impressed with how she went above and beyond to make sure this day went well for you. There is no doubt in any of our minds how much she loves you. And you know if your sisters are impressed, that is saying a lot."

"So you know what happened with our food delivery service?"

"I do," Noah nodded. "But you really don't know what she did, do you?"

"I figured she called in some favors. Rebecca is very well-connected so I have no doubts she utilized all of her resources."

His brother shook his head. "She went above and beyond," he said. "When the owner of a multimillion-dollar corporation calls me to ask whether or not I think she'd be interested in a job after she cold-called him without introduction and made such an indelible impression that speaks volumes."

Noah spent the next few minutes filling his brother in on all that he had missed. When he was done Nathaniel sat with his mouth open, stunned.

"She didn't tell me," he said, his voice a loud whisper.

"Why do you need her to tell you everything?" Naomi interjected. "You need to get over that. Or, you're going to get your feelings hurt!"

The two brothers exchanged a look, shaking their heads as Noah chuckled under his breath.

Nicholas sat on the blankets beside the two of them, having used his upper body to pull himself closer. He leaned his weight against the side of his twin brother's leg. "The girls told me you were in your feelings about Rebecca keeping secrets from you."

Nathaniel shook his head, tossing Noah a look. "You told them, didn't you?"

Noah held up his hands as if he were surrendering. "I didn't say a thing! I swear!"

Naomi laughed. "No one has to tell us anything. You three just forget how well we know you."

John Stallion added his two cents to the conversation. "Leave it alone, cousins! I can say with a fair amount of certainty that these women are using some kind of voodoo on all of us."

"Really, John Stallion? Voodoo? You can't do any better than that?"

John leaned to kiss his wife. He gave Marah a bright smile. "Honey, you know I'm just joking, right?"

It was well after midnight when the house was finally quiet, the family having left for their respective hotels. Rebecca placed the last dirty dish into the dishwasher and turned the device on. After checking one last time that all the doors and windows were locked and secure, she shut off the lights and headed toward the master bedroom.

Nathaniel was sound asleep atop the mattress. He had snatched the bedclothes from the bed and dropped them to the floor. He lay sprawled on his stomach, wrapped in the towel he'd worn from the shower. He snored loudly, finally giving in to the exhaustion that had been weighing heavily on him for most of the month.

Rebecca picked the blankets up from the floor and tossed them over his backside. Seeing him content and comfortable in a way that he had not been for a long while made her smile. He deserved the rest and she was grateful to see him find it. After she covered him she stripped out of her own clothes and headed into the bathroom. After emptying her bladder, she removed her eye makeup and washed away the last remnants of blushing foundation. After spending a few minutes massaging moisturizer into her skin, Rebecca brushed her teeth and turned on the shower to warm.

The spray of hot water felt good against her skin. She stood under the steady stream for a few good moments and reached to turn the massage head on a higher pulse. In no time at all her body was relaxed, her muscles feeling like loose jelly. Once she was lathered and rinsed, she cut off the spray of water and grabbed a towel from the rack. Minutes later she was dried, oiled, powdered and spritzed. She felt amazingly refreshed to be so tired. Back in the bedroom Nathaniel had crawled over to his side of the bed. He lay on his back staring up toward the ceiling.

"Hey, I didn't wake you, did I?" Rebecca questioned.

"No, baby, you didn't. I was only dozing."

"It certainly didn't sound like it. You were snoring up something fierce!"

Nathaniel chuckled. "You sure that wasn't you? You're the one who usually snores."

Rebecca laughed, the alto tone vibrating softly off the four walls. She crawled into the bed beside him, cradling her buttocks into the curve of his crotch. He leaned to kiss her shoulder, pressing a line of damp kisses against her skin. She smelled sweet, like the scent of the honeysuckle and vanilla bodywash that had turned up in his shower.

Since she had taken up residence in his home, he found remnants of her in the most unlikely places. Tampons were suddenly tucked in the cabinet beneath the sink. An assortment of shampoos and natural hair care products lined the marble countertops around his sink. Her clothes were intermingled with his clothes, the occasional satin chemise and matching bottom hanging beside one of his dress shirts.

Her favorite gummy fruit candies now sat in decorative jars on his kitchen countertops. Occasionally there would be jelly beans or Hershey's kisses or any other assortment of candy that excited her taste buds. He hated admitting it, but he looked forward to the treats and her unexpected presence was a pleasant reminder of how much he missed her when she was gone.

Since moving the relationship forward, making love to her all night long had become the most delightful fantasy come true. They spent hours pleasuring each other, delighting in the discoveries that gave them both much joy. Making love to Rebecca could go from slow and sweet one minute to heated and passionate and then dark and dirty depending on her mood, or his.

He felt a wave of heat twitch in his southern quadrant as he thought about her, a quiver of electricity coursing through his bloodstream. Rebecca shifted her hips against him, inciting the rise of nature pressing hard against her buttocks. Without warning he rolled her toward him, his arms pulling her close as he sucked against her bottom lip. His kissed her, their tongues meeting and playing gently together. He slid his hands into her hair and drove his tongue into her mouth as she sucked him in deeper and deeper.

His hands held her tightly, fingers pressed against her back, her soft luscious breasts kissing the hard lines of his chest. Nipples kissed nipples, the sweeping sensation of one against the other playing havoc with his nerves. He slid his hands down the length of her back as he rolled her above him. He gripped the cushion of her ass, lifting her legs so that she straddled his waist. The kissing continued, mouths teasing and tasting until his mouth moved boldly down the length of her neck; nuzzling, kissing, sucking gently on the flesh.

His hands danced across her breasts, squeezing the nipples that rolled like marbles beneath his fingertips. They hung down against him, waving sweetly before his face. He pulled her closer and licked her ear, teasing the line of flesh as he whispered her name over and over. The sweet mantra had her excited, her breathing becoming labored as she panted softly. His lips returned to her nipple, clasping it beneath his teeth. The tip of his tongue teased the fleshy tissue, lapping hungrily at her skin as he made little circles with his tongue. Rebecca inhaled sharply, low moans expressing her pleasure.

It surprised him when she suddenly spun herself around, her pelvis still grinding against him. He entered her easily in a reverse cowboy that had him wishing it never had to end. She rode him slowly, up and down, over and over, the length of his maleness teasing the door to her entrance, then plunging deep in her private channel. He gripped her ass, the full moon exposure giving him ample access to hold, slap and tease the fleshy tissue.

His body convulsed and then he shouted her name, plunging himself upward and into her. She rode him over and over, until she was too tired to even consider another ride. Rebecca rolled from him, sliding his body from hers.

He chuckled softly, his voice barely a whisper. "You do that so well," he whispered, rolling himself to face her.

She took a deep breath and then a second. "I have a good partner," she said.

"Only good?"

She smiled. "You keep practicing like you've been doing and I'm sure I'll be able to label you a master in no time."

After a good night's sleep Nathaniel rose from the bed before she did. Once showered and dressed he jotted a quick note to Rebecca and headed for the restaurant. He was early enough that he planned to stop and meet his family at the airport to say goodbye.

Although he wasn't surprised when the local police chief pulled him over at the traffic stop, he wasn't expecting that the officer would demand he go downtown to answer questions. He instinctively knew his good mood would drop straight to hell. As he was allowed to leave in his own car, the officer following closely behind him, he engaged the Bluetooth device in his vehicle to connect his cell phone and call Rebecca. When she didn't immediately answer his good mood sank into a quiet abyss.

For whatever reasons, it never failed that when she had an opportunity to sleep late, something or someone had no respect for her plans. Her phone had been ringing for the last hour, pulling her up and out of her bed. A potential client had been the first intrusion. A wrong number had been the second. The third call had been her credit card company reminding her that her payment had been due two days earlier. After answering the calls Rebecca had just given up, deciding instead to shower and dress and see if she could catch up with Nathaniel.

Rebecca had been sitting on the back deck enjoying a cup of coffee when the doorbell rang. She stole a quick glance at the watch on her wrist. The doorbell ringing at such an early hour actually surprised her. She couldn't begin to imagine who might be visiting Nathaniel at that hour of the day. All of their family should have been on planes headed home by now, so she couldn't imagine that it was one of them. And Nicholas never rang the bell, his keys more like an extension to his hand.

Just as she made it midway down the hallway, she could hear her cell phone ringing for her attention in the other room. She bit back the expletive on the tip of her tongue. It was only when she reached the door that she let the colorful verbiage fly. Jeffrey Baylor stood on the other side of the door. His broken nose was braced and taped. His eyes were blackened and the skin where he was still swollen was mottled varying shades of black and blue. She took a deep breath before opening the door just enough to have a conversation with him.

"What you doing here, Jeffrey?"

"You haven't returned any of my calls."

"So maybe you should've taken the hint that I had no interest in talking to you?"

"Your boyfriend beats me up and you won't show me the courtesy of at least calling to see how I am?"

"I didn't know anything about you being beat up. And Nathaniel wouldn't do something like that. You must be mistaken." She sensed Jeffrey trying to ascertain if she was telling the truth.

"Well, he did it. He jumped me like a wild animal. He didn't give me a chance to even defend myself."

"Why are you here?" Rebecca questioned. She stood with her hand on the doorknob and the other on her hip. Irritation seeped from her eyes. She struggled not to let her emotions get the best of her.

"I was giving you a chance to make this right, Rebecca."

"Make what right?"

"I didn't want to involve the police, but since you don't want to resolve this like adults, you leave me with no other alternative."

"Jeffrey, I'm not sure what you hope I'll do or what you expect from me, but if someone kicked your ass for being a jerk then you probably deserved it. After what you and your friend Dan did trying to sabotage Nathaniel's grand opening, I really don't much care. In fact, I hope someone kicks your ass at least once a week."

"Fine, if you want to be like that. The police finally have that boyfriend of yours downtown for questioning right now. I fully intend to press charges. So there! Let's see how that helps his new little business."

"Did you really just say *so there*? Are you two years old? And you want me to be more mature?" She shook her head. "You need to leave. I don't have anything to say to you and I really don't care what you might have to say to me."

"It didn't have to be this way, Rebecca! We could have been really good together."

"Sorry. I'm already really good with Nathaniel. Goodbye, Jeffrey."

Rebecca moved to close the front door. Jeffrey suddenly thrust his foot between the door and the frame to stop her. It was pure instinct that moved her to snatch the umbrella that rested on a hook in the entranceway and slap him in the nose with it. Jeffrey howled from the pain as he fell backward clutching his face. He howled, rage suddenly rising with a vengeance. When his foot was no longer in her way, she slammed the door closed and locked it tightly.

Literally running back to the bedroom, Rebecca grabbed her cell phone from the nightstand. She dialed 911 and waited to be helped. It was only when the emergency operator assured her help was on the way that Rebecca realized Jeffrey had gone around to the back of the house and had come through the unlocked back door. Jeffrey was suddenly standing in the entrance to her bedroom staring at her, rage shining in his eyes like bolts of lightning.

Nathaniel didn't know how long he'd been sitting in the interrogation room at the City of Carmel Police Department. Detective Mark Bruno had read him his Miranda rights before abandoning him there. The officer had insisted he wasn't under arrest and was only being held for questioning. He had been allowed to keep his cell phone and he'd placed three calls. One to Rebecca, another to his cousin Matthew's wife Katrina to ask if she knew the name of a good attorney in the area. Lorenzo had been his last call. Nathaniel was a little pricked by the fact that he'd had to leave messages for all three, not one of them answering on the other end. Now he was waiting, hoping that Lorenzo had begun the preparation for the evening dinner and that he got back in time to insure everything went smoothly for his second night of business.

He began to pace back and forth, his irritation rising. He was starting to understand how encounters with the police turned on a dime. Minutes ago, he'd been calm and ready to answer any questions thrown at him. Now he was angry that there was no respect for his time, this little stunt keeping him from what he needed to do. He could only begin to imagine the brother who worked hard for an hourly wage, losing precious compensation for no good reason whatsoever.

He sat down, stood back up, sat again, and just when he was ready to slam his fist against the door for someone's attention, it swung open, Detective Bruno and a uniformed officer moving into the room. Detective Bruno was a stocky man with hair the color of black licorice. He had piercing ice blue eyes and chiseled features that reminded Nathaniel of an old movie actor. The second officer was extremely short and thin, and looked like he might fall over if the wind blew.

"We apologize for the delay, Dr. Stallion We had another problem arise relative to this case that needed to be resolved."

Nathaniel released the deep breath he'd been holding. "If we can please get this over with, Detective. I have a business I'm running that I need to get back to."

"Oh, yes, that's right. You own that new restaurant called Dinner?"

"Yes, I do." Nathaniel was suddenly reminded of the dynamics of small-town life where everyone knew your business and everyone's business was open to scrutiny.

"Well, let's just get right to it. Do you know a young woman by the name of Rebecca Marks?"

"Yes, she's my fiancée."

"And she lives with you at your home on Scenic Road?"

Nathaniel felt his anxiety level begin to rise. This was not the line of questioning he had been expecting.

"I'm sorry but what is this about? Why are you asking me about Rebecca?"

"There was an incident at your home this morning."

Nathaniel shifted forward in his seat. His body tensed, his jaw tightening. "What kind of incident? Is Rebecca okay?" He unconsciously pulled his cell phone from his pocket and pressed the redial button for Rebecca. When she didn't answer he stood up abruptly. "Where is she? Is she okay?"

"Calm down, son," Detective Bruno said. His hand waved in the air as if he were patting something. "Ms. Marks is just fine. She's actually here. In the next room, talking to one of our female officers."

"I need to see her. Please!" he implored.

"Just a few more questions and that won't be a problem."

Nathaniel and the detective exchanged gazes until Nathaniel eased himself back into his seat. He sat, ringing his hands anxiously together.

The detective continued. "What is your relationship with Jeffrey Baylor?"

Nathaniel shook his head. "We don't have a relationship. He and my fiancée were engaged many years ago. He hasn't been able to get over the rejection."

"So has he been a problem before?"

"He has a bad habit of showing up where he's not wanted. Especially since Rebecca has been in town."

The detective nodded his head slowly. "Can you tell me what happened between you two the other night?"

"I punched him," Nicholas said matter-of-factly. "I

punched him and I told him to stay away from Rebecca."

"Are you the jealous type, Dr. Stallion?"

"I'm protective of the woman I love, Detective."

"And you feel that Mr. Baylor is a threat to her?"

"I don't trust Baylor. I know he's capable of doing some underhanded things. So yes, I believe he could be a threat to her."

The detective nodded, seeming to fall into his own thoughts. After a moment he rose up onto his feet and gestured toward the other officer. "If you would please take Dr. Stallion next door to see his fiancée."

The young man nodded and waved toward Nathaniel as he moved toward the door.

"Dr. Stallion, Mr. Baylor alleges you assaulted him without provocation. This morning he broke into your home and terrorized your fiancée. Like I said, she's fine. She was not hurt. But I do believe that Mr. Baylor's actions would've provoked any man to act in defense of his woman. Mr. Baylor is going to be charged with unlawful entry, attempted assault and a few other charges. I'll present what I know to the district attorney but I doubt highly that any charges will be levied against you. I am going to recommend that this case be thrown out. However, until then I'm going to ask that you please don't leave town."

Nathaniel gave him a slight nod. "Not a problem, Detective. Thank you. I hope you're able to stop by with your family and enjoy a meal at my restaurant sometime soon."

"I look forward to it. My wife is very excited to come see what you have to offer. I'll be honest, though. This is just all a little too fancy for me. Give me a good hotdog on a bun with some mustard, a side of fries and some slaw, and I'm a happy man"

"Well, come by and let me fix your hotdog. It'll be the best one you've ever had."

"I'm gonna hold you to that, Dr. Stallion. You have a good day now!"

Rebecca was standing in the corner of the room with her back against the wall and her arms crossed over her chest. When he stepped into the room he sensed that she had been waiting for almost as long as he had. The minute she saw him she ran and threw herself against him. She wrapped her arms around his neck and held on for dear life.

"It's okay, Bec! Everything's okay, I'm right here, baby."

Rebecca nodded, her head bobbing against his chest. "I'm okay. I really am. I just want to go home."

"What happened? They said Jeffrey broke into the house? Did that son-of-a-bitch put his hands on you?"

Rebecca nodded. "He showed up at the house talking crazy. He said you were in police custody and he was pressing charges and he was going to give me a chance to make it right. I told him to leave and when I went to close the door he tried to push his way inside. I slapped him with an umbrella and then he went around the back and let himself in."

She took a deep breath and continued. "He tried to get aggressive and he grabbed me but I was able to fight him off and then the police were there before anything really bad happened."

"You left the door unlocked?"

"I was sitting out the patio enjoying a cup of coffee when the doorbell rang. I didn't think I needed to lock the door."

"I'm going to change that door so it locks automatically when it closes."

"Oh, that'll work. I can see me locking myself out every time I want to go down to the beach! No."

"Well, maybe I didn't think that one through but we'll need to do something to keep you safe."

Rebecca signed softly. "I am so ready to leave."

"What are we waiting for?"

"Barney Fife is trying to get his ducks in a row."

Nathaniel laughed. "I thought he looked more like Ben Matlock with black hair."

"Who?"

"Matlock."

"Who's Matlock?"

Nathaniel had to laugh at the expression on her face. "You know Barney Fife but you don't know Matlock?"

"Pop culture has never been my thing."

"It's Matlock. Everyone knows Matlock!"

"Well, obviously, everyone doesn't. I don't!"

"That's what we're going to do on Monday when the restaurant's closed. We're going to lie in bed all day watching old *Matlock* episodes while I wait on you hand and foot."

"Will you make me coconut cream pie?"

"I will make you whatever your heart desires!"

"It's a date!" she said as she reached to kiss his lips.

The door to the room suddenly swung open. Detective Bruno gave them both a look. "Ms. Marks, we're not going to need anything else from you right now. I trust that you'll be in good hands with Dr. Stallion?"

Rebecca smiled politely. "I know I will be. Thank you."

"Then you both are free to leave. We'll be in touch if we need anything else from either of you."

"What will happen with Jeffrey?" Rebecca asked.

"Mr. Baylor will be held until he's officially charged and given a bail hearing. Then once he makes bond he'll be free to go until his hearing. But don't you worry, the district attorney will make sure you also get a restraining order so you won't have to worry about him bothering you."

"Thank you," Nathaniel said. He pressed his hand against the small of her back.

Rebecca gave the man another smile. As they headed out the door, she muttered under her breath. "Does he even have a clue that a restraining order is rarely worth the ink on the paper? How many men have violated their restraining orders, leaving law enforcement apologizing after someone's been hurt, or worse?"

Nathaniel reflected on her comment. He knew her well enough that she was trying to deflect from her own fear. He had no doubt that Jeffrey's behavior had scared her and she was trying not to let him see it. He drew a calming hand down her back, the warmth of his touch healing.

"I promise, everything is going to be fine. I will never let anything happen to you, Bec. Now let's just get you home!"

Chapter 14

After a busy weekend at the restaurant Nathaniel and Rebecca were both looking forward to a quiet day together. Sleeping in late that Monday morning had felt like a long-lost luxury and both relished being able to share the moment together.

He'd awakened to Rebecca tasting him, her lush lips gliding up and down over his morning erection. The sensations she elicited from his body had left him shivering, every muscle in his body firing with a vengeance. He'd lost count of the number of times they had orgasmed together. Only that by the time they were hungry for lunch both could barely walk.

He stood in the kitchen preparing their first meal of the day. Rebecca was still in the shower, hoping the cold water would revive her senses. He was plating their steak and eggs when Rebecca finally found her way to the kitchen.

"I was just about to send in the troops after you, Bec!"

"That water felt good. Even when it went cold!"

He smiled as he gestured for her to take a seat. "We need to make some decisions, Bec."

"What decisions?"

"Where we plan to live? When you want to get married? How soon before we start thinking about a family? Nothing major."

She smiled as she took a bite of her steak. "I'm not selling my condo. In case this doesn't work out I need to know I have a home to go back to."

"Really?" He eyed her over the tops of his reading glasses."

"I'm being practical. A girl can't be too careful these days."

Nathaniel laughed. "I can't with you sometimes, Rebecca Marks!"

She grinned. "But you'll be doing it with me, and only me, for the rest of your life. I hope you're ready for that."

He wrapped his arms around her shoulders and hugged her to him. "I am more ready than you will ever know!"

They made plans as they enjoyed their meal. They talked about a future that held dreams and expectations, desires that the two of them would only share with each other.

"How do you feel about dogs?" Rebecca asked. "Because I would really like a dog one day."

"As long as it's not one of those little yippy dogs you kick, I'm good."

"You'd kick a little dog?"

"They get under your feet and you can't help it! It's not like I'd be kicking it on purpose. Not often anyway!"

Rebecca laughed. "That is wrong in so many ways!"

He kissed her cheek as he reached for her empty plate. "Wrong but true."

She slid off her stool, gathering the rest of the dirty dishes to help him clean up the mess. It took no time at all before they had the kitchen back in its neat and orderly fashion.

"Did I tell you today that I love you?" Nathaniel asked.

"I don't think you did," she said as she put the last clean plates into the cabinet.

He started to hum, putting eggs and butter back into the refrigerator. They settled into the silence for a few good minutes.

"So what happened?" Rebecca questioned.

"Excuse me?"

"Weren't you going to tell me that you love me?"

"Oh, that! I was going to save it for later. I don't want you to get spoiled thinking I should say it more than once per day."

Rebecca laughed, the wealth of it vibrating through her midsection. "You better be glad I like you!"

He moved to where she was standing and wrapped himself around her in a warm embrace. "Our liking each other is why we found it so easy to love each other. And I love you, Rebecca Marks. I love everything about you."

"Even my stretch marks?"

"I love them," he said with a wink of his eye as he tapped her on the ass.

The moment was suddenly interrupted by the ring of the doorbell.

"Are you expecting someone?" Rebecca asked as she pulled her bathrobe closed around her curves.

He shook his head. "No," he responded as he headed in the direction of the front door. He took a quick look through the peephole then tossed Rebecca a look over his shoulder.

"It's Elise," he whispered.

Rebecca gave him an eye roll. "That's your problem," she whispered loudly. "I'll be in the bedroom."

"You're just going to leave me?"

"You bet your bippy!"

"What the hell's a bippy?"

"I don't have a clue. I heard one of your nieces say it. I thought it would make me sound cool."

Nathaniel laughed. "It doesn't," he said as he reached for the door handle.

Elise was smiling, her real estate grin saying hello. "Nathaniel! I hope this isn't a bad time?"

He stepped aside, smiling politely. "Elise, it's good to see you. How have you been?"

"I've been great. I just thought you might be interested to know that Jeffrey Baylor has put his restaurant on the market for sale. You might not be ready to invest in a second property at the moment, but it's definitely something you may want to consider down the road. Especially since I hear that the restaurant is doing very well. Congratulations on your success! I hate that I was out of town for your grand opening."

"Well, thank you. I hope to see you there some time soon. I owe you a dinner for everything you've done for me."

Elise gave him her brightest smile. "Well, I might have to hold you to that!"

Nathaniel nodded. "Please do. I'm sorry to hear about Jeffrey. Will he be leaving Carmel?"

"Apparently he's decided to go back to Europe. To try and make things work with his wife and kids."

"Wife?"

"I was told they had filed for divorce but stopped it. I'm not quite sure and you know I'm not one to gossip!" she said with a spry laugh.

"Not you!" Nathaniel said teasingly.

"You could invite a girl in for a drink," she said, her brow shifting as if she had something caught in her eye.

Nathaniel shook his head. "We're not doing this again, Elise. I can't."

"I wasn't implying anything, Nathaniel. I just thought

you might have something to quench a girl's parched throat."

Nathaniel hesitated for a brief moment and then he turned, moving toward the kitchen. He grabbed a clean glass from the cabinet and filled it with ice and water from the refrigerator door. Turning back toward the foyer he was surprised to find her sitting on the edge of his sofa, posing seductively with a come-hither stare.

He was just about to say something when Rebecca came through the door. His eyes widened as he caught sight of her. She'd changed into a high-waisted lace-and-sequined panty and tasseled pasties that covered the nipples of her breasts and little else. A sexy, strappy high-heel completed her ensemble. She carried a red and black leather flogger, looking like an advertisement for Dominatrix-R-Us.

She strutted casually into the space, moving toward the sound system and turning on the stereo. "Elise, hey! How are you? You're just in time! Will you be staying long?"

Else jumped from her seat looking like she'd fallen headfirst into the rabbit hole. "No…um… Rebecca… I…hey…"

Rebecca cracked her whip at her side, leaning on one hip. She stared at the woman and licked her lips.

"I was just leaving!" Elise said, practically racing for the door.

"Don't rush off," Rebecca responded. "I was just about to show Nathaniel a good time." She snapped that whip one last time.

They both moved to the door to see her out, watching as she practically raced down the driveway to her car. Rebecca cut her eye in Nathaniel's direction, her smirk spreading canyon-wide across her face.

Nathaniel burst out laughing, the wealth of it gut-deep and bringing tears to his eyes. He swiped at the moisture with the back of his hand.

"You know that wasn't right, don't you?"

She shrugged. "I don't think we'll have to worry about Elise dropping by unannounced ever again. And I think she's done with trying to turn you to the dark side."

He was still laughing. He eased an arm around her waist and pulled her close. One hand teased a single pastie, his index finger flicking it from side to side. "I really do love you!" he exclaimed.

Rebecca laughed with him. "I love you, too!"

He licked his lips. "So…um…is there something you want to tell me?" he asked, sliding his index finger beneath the leg of her panty.

Rebecca smiled, then she snapped that whip one more time before pressing her mouth to his.

* * * * *

COMING NEXT MONTH
Available March 20, 2018

#565 STILL LOVING YOU
The Grays of Los Angeles • by Sheryl Lister

Malcolm Gray is Lauren Emerson's biggest regret. Eight years ago, a lack of trust cost her a future with the star running back. Now an opportunity brings the nutrition entrepreneur home, where she hopes to declare a truce. But their first encounter unleashes explosive passion. Is this their second chance?

#566 SEDUCED IN SAN DIEGO
Millionaire Moguls • by Reese Ryan

There's nothing conventional about artist Jordan Jace, except his membership to the exclusive Millionaire Moguls. And when he meets marketing consultant Sasha Charles, persuading the straitlaced beauty to break some rules is an irresistible challenge. But their affair may be temporary, unless they can discover the art of love—together…

#567 ONE UNFORGETTABLE KISS
The Taylors of Temptation • by A.C. Arthur

All navy pilot Garrek Taylor ever wanted was to fly far from his family's past. But with his wings temporarily clipped, he's back in his hometown. His plans are sidetracked when he wins a date with unconventional house restorer Harper Presley. Will their combustible connection lead to an everlasting future?

#568 A BILLIONAIRE AFFAIR
Passion Grove • by Niobia Bryant

Alessandra Dalmount has been groomed to assume the joint reins of her father's empire. Now that day has arrived, forcing her to work closely with co-CEO and childhood nemesis Alek Ansah. As they battle for control of the billion-dollar conglomerate, can they turn their rivalry into an alliance of love?

Get 2 Free Books,

Plus 2 Free Gifts—
just for trying the
Reader Service!

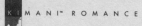

SPECIAL EXCERPT FROM

Malcolm Gray is Lauren Emerson's biggest regret. Eight years ago, a lack of trust cost her a future with the star running back. Now an opportunity brings the nutrition entrepreneur home, where she hopes to declare a truce. But their first encounter unleashes explosive passion…and unwanted memories of the precious dreams they once shared. As they jockey for position, a new set of rules could change the game for both of them…

Read on for a sneak peek at
STILL LOVING YOU,
the next exciting installment in the
THE GRAYS OF LOS ANGELES *series by Sheryl Lister!*

Mr. Green stood, helped her with her chair and waved at someone. "I know you're still meeting with players, but have you had a chance to meet Malcolm Gray yet?"

The hairs stood up on the back of her neck. Before she could respond, she felt the heat and, without turning around, knew it was Malcolm.

"Congratulations, Malcolm," Mr. Green said, shaking Malcolm's hand. "Have you met Lauren Emerson? She's going to be a great asset to the team."

Malcolm stared down into Lauren's eyes. "Thanks, and yes, we've met. Hello, Lauren."

That's one way to describe it. "Hi, Malcolm." She had only seen photos of him wearing a tuxedo, and those pictures hadn't come close to capturing the raw magnetism he exuded standing next to her. She couldn't decide whether she liked him better with his locs or the close-cropped look he now sported.

"Well, my wife is going to have my head if we don't get at least one dance in, so I'll see you two later. Malcolm, can you make sure Lauren gets acquainted with everyone?"

Lauren's eyes widened. "Oh, I'll be fine. I'm sure Malcolm has some other people to see." She looked to Malcolm, expecting him to agree. To her amazement, he extended his arm.

"Shall we?"

With Mr. Green and his wife staring at her with huge smiles, she couldn't very well say what she wanted. Instead, she took his arm and let him lead her out to the dance floor. She regretted it the moment he wrapped his arm around her. Malcolm kept a respectable distance, but it didn't matter. His closeness caused an involuntary shiver to pass through her. And why did he have to smell so good? The fragrance had a perfect balance of citrus and earth that was as comforting as it was sensual. How was she going to make it through the next five minutes?

Malcolm must have sensed her nervousness. "Relax, Lauren. We've danced closer than this, so what's the problem?"

Lauren didn't need any reminders of how close they'd been in the past. "I'm fine," she mumbled.

A minute went by and Malcolm said, "Smile. You don't want everyone to think you're not enjoying my company."

She glared up at him. "You're enjoying this, aren't you?"

He grinned. "I'm holding a beautiful woman in my arms. What's not to enjoy?"

Mr. Green and his wife smiled Lauren's way, and she smiled back. As soon as they turned away, she dropped her smile. "I can't play these games with you, Malcolm," she whispered harshly.

"This is no game." Their eyes locked for a lengthy moment, then he pulled her closer and kept up the slow sway.

Don't miss STILL LOVING YOU by Sheryl Lister, available April 2018 wherever Harlequin® Kimani Romance™ books and ebooks are sold.

Want to give in to temptation with
steamy tales of irresistible desire?

Check out **Harlequin® Presents®**,
Harlequin® Desire and
Harlequin® Kimani™ Romance books!

New books available every month!

CONNECT WITH US AT:

Harlequin.com/Community

 Facebook.com/HarlequinBooks

 Twitter.com/HarlequinBooks

 Instagram.com/HarlequinBooks

 Pinterest.com/HarlequinBooks

ReaderService.com

**ROMANCE WHEN
YOU NEED IT**

PGENRE2017

LOVE
Harlequin
romance?

Join our Harlequin community to share your thoughts and connect with other romance readers!

Be the first to find out about promotions, news, and exclusive content!

Sign up for the Harlequin e-newsletter and download a free book from any series at

www.TryHarlequin.com

CONNECT WITH US AT:

Harlequin.com/Community

 Facebook.com/HarlequinBooks

 Twitter.com/HarlequinBooks

 Instagram.com/HarlequinBooks

 Pinterest.com/HarlequinBooks

ReaderService.com

**ROMANCE WHEN
YOU NEED IT**

HSOCIAL2017